"We need to move further down so we can get to the cabin without being seen," TJ said.

"But the water is freezing."

"We won't be in it for long." He scanned the shoreline as they floated for the safest route back up to the cabin. "I've got you." TJ took her hand in his. "Just don't let go."

TJ fought against the river with all his strength, keeping Leila's head above water as he aimed for the shore. A large branch hung low over the water. TJ reached out, his fingers brushed the rough bark and he fought to get a solid grip.

"Climb up." He boosted her onto the branch, then pulled himself up. They weren't safe yet. Their attacker could still be out there.

"We need to move," TJ said, helping Leila to her feet. "Can you make it to shore?"

Leila nodded. "I'll manage. Let's go."

They made their way to the pebbled riverbank. The crunch of tires on gravel sounded above them.

TJ held up a hand. "Wait." As they scrambled for cover in the underbrush, their ordeal was far from over.

The night was dark, they were wet and freezing, and somewhere out there, a killer continued to hunt them...

Shannon Redmon remembers the first grown-up book she checked out from the neighborhood bookmobile. A Victoria Holt novel, with romance, intrigue and ballroom parties, captivated her attention and flamed her desire to write. She hopes her stories immerse readers in a world of joy and escape while encouraging faith, hope and love for those around us. Shannon is represented by Tamela Hancock Murray of the Steve Laube Agency.

Books by Shannon Redmon

Love Inspired Suspense

Cave of Secrets
Secrets Left Behind
Mistaken Mountain Abduction
Christmas Murder Cover-Up
Unraveling Killer Secrets
Mountain Murder Threat

Visit the Author Profile page at LoveInspired.com.

MOUNTAIN MURDER THREAT

SHANNON REDMON

LOVE INSPIRED SUSPENSE
INSPIRATIONAL ROMANCE

LOVE INSPIRED® SUSPENSE
INSPIRATIONAL ROMANCE

ISBN-13: 978-1-335-63885-4

Mountain Murder Threat

Love Inspired
22 Adelaide St. West, 41st Floor
Toronto, Ontario M5H 4E3, Canada
www.LoveInspired.com

Printed in Lithuania

Recycling programs for this product may not exist in your area.

MIX
Paper | Supporting responsible forestry
FSC® C021394

For God, who commanded the light to shine
out of darkness, hath shined in our hearts,
to give the light of the knowledge of the glory of God
in the face of Jesus Christ.
—*2 Corinthians* 4:6

To all my author friends—
you are an inspiration to me. Thank you
for all your support through the years. Love you all!

ONE

Detective Leila Kane's footsteps slapped the asphalt as she leaned her body into the familiar curves of her subdivision. Four a.m. came early and the seventy-degree weather she'd basked in just a few days ago had turned frigid again. Typical for March. The crisp air bit at her exposed skin, and she pulled her lightweight running jacket tighter around her body.

The weatherman on Channel Five had warned of an impending snowstorm when she was putting on her shoes this morning. Could be as severe as the one over thirty years ago. Not that she remembered, since she was a baby then, but her mother had kept pictures of her sisters playing in the piles of snow. According to Holly, her oldest sister, they didn't have to go to school for a week. The thought of such carefree days brought a wistful smile to Leila's face.

What she wouldn't give to be an innocent child again, but Leila didn't have that luxury now. Her mind rolled with details of her current homicide case. The victim's face kept appearing in her mind's eye, those lifeless eyes seeming to plead for justice. She'd hoped a run in fresh air and colder temperatures would clear away the clutter, but so far nothing had helped.

Maybe if she focused on her present surroundings the answers would emerge. With an inhale, her senses sharpened—fresh-cut hay from the pasture across the street, wisps of smoke from her neighbor's chimney, and the rich scent of roasted coffee from the local breakfast truck at the end of the block reminded her she needed caffeine. The aroma made her mouth water and her stomach growled in response.

Mackey's Brewhouse poured the best coffee in the area and every day on her way to work she stopped for a caffeinated jolt of energy. Maybe that would help sharpen her mental acuity regarding her victim's killer. She'd finish her run, then grab a to-go cup, hoping the familiar routine would help ground her. No pun intended.

Her team struggled to uncover any leads despite the fact they'd been working for three weeks. Other cases were piling up even though she'd solved the last homicide rather quickly. Easy to do when the doggie cam captured the entire horrifying event. Poor guy never expected to come home and get shot ten times by his jilted lover. The memory of that case made her shudder, the images still vivid in her mind.

But her current case was not coming together. The young female victim, Stacy Greene, had been abducted from Peony Street in Leila's neighborhood. Nothing unusual stood out in the victim's background—happily married, two dogs, a great career and left her husband a sweet voice message the day she was abducted. No sign of any problems at home or work. No evidence of an affair or financial problems. Her husband had reported her missing within the appropriate amount of time and they'd found her body three days later—strangled and dumped a mile off the Blue Ridge Parkway, near Wildcat Falls.

An uneasy feeling nagged her on this one. The evidence was sparse, the motive almost nonexistent and the killer left behind few leads—the makings for a cold case. There had to be something they were missing, some detail that would crack the case open or at least point them in the right direction. Right now, all the details seemed random and provided no path to even a possible theory.

Leila harnessed her frustration and pushed until her legs burned, ascending the final hill. Her house was just on the other side. This was always the hardest section but the most rewarding. The last part of the run gave her the boost of adrenaline she needed for most days.

As she kicked up her regular pace a notch, her ponytail swished and slapped against her back. The sprint to the top didn't come easy but she'd learned nothing good in life ever did. Once she finished the entire course, today's routine coasted downhill from there. She pushed herself harder, her breath coming in short, sharp bursts.

The hum of an engine echoed behind her and headlights cast her elongated shadow onto the asphalt. She slowed, then shifted to the sidewalk to give the driver room. A black sedan passed on her right. The man in the driver's seat gave a slight wave although she didn't see who was inside. Probably a third shift worker from the local plant headed home for a good day's sleep. The car turned down a side road and his red taillights faded into the curves and turns of her neighborhood.

A lone dog barked, igniting other neighborhood howlers to join him. The hairs on Leila's neck bristled. She'd always been one to pay attention to her surroundings, especially nature. Birds, horses and other animals knew when disaster was about to strike before humans even had a clue. Dogs especially were keen and she'd always wanted to get one, but her job required so much that she wasn't sure she had enough energy left over at the end of the day to give to something else. Another reason she and her ex-boyfriend, TJ, didn't work out.

She glanced over her shoulder. No one was around. Not sure why she had an uneasy feeling twisting in her gut. Something seemed off this morning. Maybe it was just her. She'd not been sleeping well either and long days at work viewing gruesome details could take a toll on one's mental health. The shadows seemed to loom larger, the silence more oppressive.

Leila tried to shrug off the nagging feeling of paranoia, increased her pace and focused on the last stretch of road cloaked by dark woods on each side. The trees seemed to reach out with gnarled branches, creating eerie shapes in the predawn gloom. She shook her head, trying to dispel the morbid imagery her tired mind conjured up.

A car door slammed from the side street where the sedan had turned. She glanced down the dark road but there were no lights or movement to provide any insight. Probably the same guy heading inside to his family. She needed to get a grip. After all, she was a cop and could take care of herself. Still, her hand instinctively moved to her hip, where her service weapon would normally be. But this was just a morning run; she wasn't armed.

Her home was just ahead on the left and her outdoor patio light cast a soft glow into the fog. Her eerie feelings began to fade as the familiar sight of her house came into view. Why was she so nervous? This was a safe neighborhood and there was nothing to fear. She tried to convince herself of this, but a part of her remained on high alert.

A loud rumble shattered through the early morning silence. Leila swiveled her gaze toward the noise. A burgundy van barreled straight toward her from the same side street. Twin headlights blinded her vision and fumes of diesel twisted in a thick cloud of black exhaust. She tried to move, but other than her heart pounding inside her chest, she stood frozen, the silver grill on the van's nose charging toward her at full force.

Time seemed to slow down as Leila's training kicked in. She jumped back, catching the curb with her foot. Cold, wet grass softened her fall but pain shot through her back when she landed. Her fingers dug into the dirt and she scrambled to get out of the way, fleeing the impact. The van's tires screeched to halt mere inches from where she had been standing. The metal door scraped open and a man emerged—tall with dark eyes shadowed by a black hoodie and a dark scarf tied around his face. He charged toward her without a word, his intentions clear in the predatory way he moved.

Leila's mind raced.

This was it.

This was how so many of the victims she'd investigated met their end. Caught off guard, alone, vulnerable and unarmed. But she wasn't going to go down without a fight. She was a detective, trained to handle situations like this. Or so she thought.

Leila ran but his python grasp circled her body and tightened. She couldn't move or scream as his hand clamped over her mouth and nose, smothering her ability to breathe. The face of her female victim flashed through her mind. If she didn't fight, she'd be the next one on her team's missing wall.

The man shoved her toward the open van door, keeping a firm hold. Leila leaned against his chest, planted her foot against the side of the van and shoved her body backward. The jarring motion knocked him off balance and he fell to the ground, taking her with him. She landed on his chest, then rolled to the side, the skunky scent of his clothes searing into her mind.

He grabbed for her but she managed to get away, landing a swift kick to his head. He curled into a ball as she raced up the hill toward her neighbor's house. No lights were on but if she could get inside, she could find a way to defend herself. Her lungs burned as she gulped in the cold morning air, her legs protesting the sudden sprint after her long run.

With a glance back, she saw that the man was on his feet, chasing her—approximately five-ten and two hundred pounds. He was a solid build but she'd be faster if she could just push through the burning in her legs. Adrenaline coursed through her muscles and she pumped her arms, to fuel the race up the steep incline.

Leila reached her neighbor's porch railing but her head jerked back as her pursuer grasped her ponytail. Her body followed. Pain seared through the side of her head when his fist connected with her temple. Stars exploded in her vision and her knees buckled.

He pulled her backward and she teetered, arms flailing, desperate to regain her balance. But the momentum was too much. She tumbled down the steep embankment, leaves and twigs whipping at her face as she fell.

Tree trunks and stones beat against her as she rolled, each impact a sickening thud against her flesh. Finally, she landed in the dried-up creek bed at the bottom, dazed and unable to move. Everything hurt. She tried to sit up but the throb in her head kept her still. The world spun around her, and for a moment, she wasn't sure which way was up.

Footsteps crunched through the forest debris. If she didn't run, he would finish what he'd started. But before she could escape, his hulking silhouette emerged in her blurred vision, looming over her. The shadows seemed to cling to him, making him appear more monster than man.

He dropped to his knees, next to her body and hoisted her up, wrapping an arm around her throat and squeezing tight as he dragged her body back up the embankment. Leila fought against him. It was no use: he outmatched her in sheer brute strength. What little fight she had, drained from her body as his iron grip cut off her airflow.

Dark spots crept into the edges of her vision, blocking out the crime about to happen. She'd be another statistic. Another victim. The irony wasn't lost on her—a detective becoming the very thing she'd spent her career trying to prevent.

If that were the case, then she'd give her team what they needed to find this guy. Leila dug her nails into the killer's arm, determined to gather enough DNA for identification. If she was going to die, then she'd sacrifice her life to help more women. Her last homage to the brave men and women who fought to protect their communities from crimes like this.

Her consciousness began to slip away and the faces of the ones Leila loved most flashed through her mind—her parents, her sisters, her colleagues… TJ. She'd fought for so many victims and their families to provide them with closure. Would the people she loved get answers or be left in the dark like her current victim, the one whose killer she'd failed to catch. In that moment, Leila made a silent vow. If she survived this, she would never stop fighting. She would catch this criminal, and make sure he never hurt anyone again.

The dark sky above her lightened, then bounced through the trees, highlighting the green canopy above her. This wasn't the eternal light she'd heard so much about from stories of those who had survived death. The light beam flashing around her grew brighter and closer. Muffled shouts echoed through the air.

The assailant's grip loosened, his gaze focused on someone behind her. She couldn't see anyone's face but this was her opening. With every last ounce of strength, she landed a strong blow to the man's knee. He released her completely, clutched his leg and limped up the other side of the embankment to escape.

Leila dropped to the ground, gasping for the cool air to fill her lungs. A shadowed figure drew closer. She tried to speak, to tell them about the attacker, but her voice came out as a raspy whisper.

"Don't let him get away."

She pointed in the direction of her attacker but he didn't listen. He knelt by her side instead, backlit by the moon. Was he friend or foe? She blinked to bring his features into focus but everything around her faded.

Officer TJ Snowe savored the scent of steaming coffee as he stood outside Mackey's

Brewhouse, one of two food trucks located in Shadow Creek's largest subdivision. The early morning was cold. More like winter than early spring.

"You want the usual?" Mackey, the owner, asked.

"Yeah. Thanks. Make it a large. I'm going to need the extra heat today."

"Where's that cute girl of yours that used to come with you?"

"We're not together anymore."

"Well, I guess that explains why you're getting your coffee at this location instead of my other truck on the west side." Mackey poured an extra espresso shot into his cup.

"It's fine," TJ said. "We're still friends. Still work together. I just like my mornings without the reminder that we couldn't make our relationship work."

Mackey handed him his coffee. "An extra shot to help with your morning boost."

TJ ran a hand through his hair. "Thanks. It was a long, boring night."

"Can't say I envy you. I like to be busy." He handed TJ some napkins and a lid.

"Thanks." He took a sip. "Hey, how long have you had this location open now?"

"About six months. Why?"

"You ever see anything suspicious in the neighborhood, like people skulking around the houses or neighborhood when they shouldn't be."

"Not that I've noticed but I can keep an eye out for ya if you want."

"That would be great. Thanks. See you tomorrow."

TJ walked toward his car, sipping his hot beverage and savoring the flavor. Best coffee in the area. He slipped into his driver's seat all while scanning the streets for any illicit activity. The recent spate of burglaries and assaults between 3 a.m. to 6 a.m. had left the community on edge, and with the elusive culprits one step ahead of law enforcement, all patrol units were on high alert for anything remotely suspicious.

The next strike was inevitable since no break-ins had been reported in almost two weeks now. That was the typical span of time between each incident but with only thirty minutes left in his shift, he figured today wasn't going to be eventful.

So far the thieves excelled at this cat and mouse game their team had played for three months. Somehow they always seemed to escape without detection.

A call crackled through his radio. "All units, Dispatch, we have a possible 10-35 at 52 Harwood Road."

TJ leaned into the console and cranked up the volume on his radio with the news of a major crime alert. That was Leila's address. He punched the button to engage the SUV's blue lights and siren, tearing out of the coffee truck lot into a labyrinth of paved streets, roundabouts and four-way stop signs.

Despite the short distance and his intimate knowledge of the neighborhood, each block felt like a never-ending stretch of road, the weight of the situation pressing on his chest. Just because he had ended things with Leila several months ago, it didn't mean his emotions had vanished. Their shared future might have crumbled, but the thought of any harm coming to her filled him with a dread he knew he couldn't bear.

TJ pulled up behind her sedan in the driveway, the scene seemingly undisturbed. He approached the front door and knocked, but there was no answer. The house seemed secure and the windows were closed.

He made his way back toward the road as a golf cart approached with Leila seated beside the driver. The security guard introduced himself as Pete Bell and extended his hand toward him.

"Nice to meet you."

TJ sized up the man—about six feet tall, 180 pounds, green eyes and dark hair buzzed cut—and then shifted his gaze to Leila. "Are you okay? What happened?"

She shrugged. TJ leaned down to get a better assessment, but the top of the cart shadowed her face. She held a gauze pad against the side of her head.

"She's got a pretty good gash and can't remember much," Pete said, stepping from the driver's side. He motioned up the hill. "I found her at the bottom of that embankment back there, fighting with a large guy. When I shouted at him, he ran, hopped into a dark burgundy van and left. I got his license plate tag. HJR 007. Thought you might want that."

The man stood a little straighter, clearly proud of his prowess.

TJ typed the tag info into his phone then held out his hand to Leila, whose cold fingers slipped into his palm. She stood and lowered the bandage from her head. The glow from the streetlight highlighted her injuries. "Thanks for coming."

"Kind of my job."

A shy smile turned up the corners of her mouth. "I guess so."

He motioned to her wound. "Need to keep pressure on that to stop the bleeding."

"Right."

The gash looked deep and her face was pale. Purple bruises circled her neck. Whoever attacked her had tried to strangle her. A protective rage rushed through TJ's body. He'd hunt down the man who did this to her and make him pay. Violence against women was unacceptable and he'd lived with too much of it growing up to tolerate any abusive man now. "We need to get someone to check you out."

"Probably." Leila leaned against the golf cart, her body shivering with cold.

He radioed for the paramedics as more officers arrived within seconds. One roped off the crime scene while the other took the security guard's statement.

"Let's get you inside." He nodded toward her home. "I've got a trauma bag in the car and we can at least bandage that cut while we wait for the paramedics to get here. Won't hurt you to warm up a bit too."

Without protest, she followed him toward his car as he grabbed the trauma bag from the back then entered her house.

A cozy warmth enveloped TJ as soon as they walked inside. Flames flickered from the fireplace and the fan hummed, blowing heat into the room. One lamp cast a faint glow in the open space.

TJ made his way to the kitchen to fix her some hot tea, not even pausing to ask where the mugs were. He knew. After all, they'd dated for two years and had planned to marry in June.

Until she got the detective job over him. He tried to be supportive but the tension between them increased with all the extra cases and long hours she worked. They hardly had time for each other, deteriorating their relationship to the point of calling it quits. Probably for the best. He wasn't marriage material anyway.

The teakettle's whistle interrupted his thoughts. He poured two cups with the steaming water and made his way back into the living room, taking a look at the cut on her head again when he stood near her. "I think you're going to need stitches."

She took the mug from his hands. "I've got some airplane glue in the drawer. We can use that with a butterfly bandage for now."

"That will fix the gash, but what about the bruises on your neck? Sergeant Quinn will demand you get a full assessment."

Her fingers rubbed the area. "I know."

TJ set his cup on a coaster and pulled the cleaning supplies from his bag, then applied the betadine. Leila flinched with the pressure.

"Sorry." He lightened his touch. "So, can you tell me what happened?"

Her lips thinned into a line. "I don't remember much."

"What about the guy who attacked you? Remember him?"

"Just his eyes. Dark and intense."

"Anything else?"

Leila moved away from his hand and rested her head back against a pillow. "Unfortunately, no, and I think he could be tied to another case I'm working. I can't believe I let him get away."

"This man launched a surprise attack on you. I'm thankful you're alive."

She didn't respond, her fingers still touching her neck.

"Walk me through what you do remember," TJ said.

"I was on my routine jog coming down the stretch of road to my house." She took a sip of her tea as he adhered the butterfly strips. "A van came from the side road. I jumped out of the way and ran for the neighbor's house but he got out of his van and chased me. He hit me."

"With the van?"

"No. With his fist." She pointed to her head. "And that's when everything gets fuzzy. Especially his face."

"What about his build? Height and—"

The doorbell rang. TJ stood. "That's probably the paramedics."

A burst of chill wind swept into the foyer as TJ opened the door. He crossed his arms against the onslaught of the weatherman's cold front and stepped onto her front porch.

No one was there. Instead, a small brown package sat on Leila's white railing. Had that been when they entered and he didn't see it? Delivery services didn't typically run this early in the morning.

Maybe she'd overnighted something. "Were you expecting a delivery?" TJ yelled back over his shoulder.

"No. Why?"

He pulled a pair of vinyl gloves from his pocket, slipped them on and lifted the package from the railing before returning inside. "Because this was on the porch for you."

She held out her hand. "I guess I've ordered something although I don't remember what."

He handed her a pair of gloves. "Just in case you didn't and this is evidence."

She slipped on the protection, then took the box, ripping off the perforated cardboard strip. Leila flipped open the lid and pulled out a smaller red box. Inside was a silver army lapel pin with a parachute in the middle and wings spread out to the side.

"I know I didn't order blood wings."

"Blood wings?" TJ looked closer.

"It's a tradition or initiation process some in the military use after a soldier completes their training where the pin is pounded into the chest, drawing blood. The practice has been outlawed but apparently some units still keep to the tradition. My father used to tell the story. In fact, I think Mom still has his pin in a case with the flag that was draped over his coffin."

TJ placed a hand to his chest. "That sounds painful."

"It is but it also creates a bond between the soldiers in the unit. At least that's what Dad told me. He was a paratrooper and jumped out of airplanes a lot. His entire unit was blood pinned."

"May I take a closer look?"

Leila handed him the box. "This is the same pin my victim had attached to her when we found her body at Wildcat Falls."

"In her chest?" TJ took the box from her fingers to view the details.

"Yeah. He must've punched it to her right before he killed her. There were traces of her blood on the back."

"We could track down the manufacturer."

"I've already been down that rabbit hole. They sell them on the internet. Anyone could order one from dozens of manufacturers. It's like trying to find a needle in the proverbial haystack."

"You think our killer is military?"

"Or wants us to think he is, if this is even from him. Since this looks like my dad's pin, I'm going to text Mom and rule out that she sent this to me. I don't want to assume this is from the man who attacked me today if my mother decided to ship me something of my father's." Leila pulled out her phone and tapped the screen.

TJ turned the pin over and over in his gloved hand, trying to memorize every detail. "Can I ask you something personal?"

"Shoot."

"How did your father pass away again?"

"Six months ago, he had a stroke while in the hospital. Dad had heart issues, atrial fibrillation to be exact which caused his stroke.

When he was stable they moved him to the rehab hospital since he still needed a lot of physical and occupational therapy to regain the use of his muscles and learn how to live with his new restrictions. The day after he was admitted to rehab, they found him on the floor with a gash on his head. They think he tried to walk to the bathroom without a nurse, had a stroke and fell. He died the next day."

"I guess we have that in common. Both our fathers gone."

Her phone buzzed. "Mom didn't send me anything."

She reached for the box.

TJ placed the pin inside, closed the lid and handed the potential evidence to her. "Then this is most likely related to your attack."

"Agreed." Her phone chimed again and she tapped out another message. "I'll make sure it gets logged into evidence so I can compare it to my victim's pin."

Her phone chimed a third time. "I shouldn't have asked her anything about this. Now she has all kinds of questions." Leila continued to type.

"Only serial killers mark their victims," TJ said, the words almost sticking in his throat. The thought of a serial killer targeting Leila tensed every muscle in his body.

"Yeah." She stood, walked to a bench by the door, and retrieved a plastic bag from her backpack, then pushed the box inside.

She returned to him, holding out her phone. "Here's a photo of the same pin on the victim from my current case."

The gray pallor of the woman's skin paled in comparison to the darker colored pin tacked to her chest. TJ snapped a couple of photos. "If he is a serial killer, then you're his next target."

TJ handed the phone back to her and Leila turned away as if she didn't want to think about the ramifications that her attacker could be a serial killer. "We can't make that claim yet, not without another body and the medical examiner's input."

"I'm going to take my trauma bag back to the car and check to see why the paramedics aren't here yet." He stood. "You should rest. I'll be back in a few."

The cold wind whipped against him when he exited her home. This winter season had been frigid but dry. Not one good snowfall this year, even in the high mountains. Now, the news was predicting a large storm for later this week. He hoped for at least a foot of accumulation to help keep everyone off the streets and safe inside their homes.

TJ popped the rear door and placed the bag inside. Several dogs barked in the distance. He glanced around the large neighborhood, wondering where Leila's attacker might be now. Was he watching from a distance or headed back to his home base?

Flashing red lights crossed the top of the hill and moved toward Leila's home. Finally, the paramedics were here. Once they took a look at her, he'd talk to the neighbors and collect security camera footage. Someone had to have seen something.

A fierce protection rose up within TJ. He'd do everything in his power to keep Leila safe despite the fact that she had broken his heart. If they could put the past behind them and work together, they might stop this killer from hurting anyone else. Then he could get back to his daily life without the reminder that Leila was the one that got away.

TWO

The emergency room had been crowded and as news traveled through the precinct's gossip mill, several of her colleagues stopped by, including Sergeant Quinn. He wanted details but her memory didn't provide much. Leila was thankful to be headed home, twelve hours later.

She glanced over at TJ driving the SUV. His conversation with Sergeant Quinn at the hospital had been cryptic at best, which was never good. They had talked about her but she was excluded from the conversation. Like she wasn't even there. She understood everyone wanting to protect her but what she really needed was help finding her attacker.

He shot her a nervous smile. "Quinn wants us to set up a protection detail."

She didn't like the idea but figured she didn't have a choice. "Okay."

"And he wants to talk to you about handing over your homicide case to Detective Edwards."

"Are you kidding me? I've put so many hours of work into that case. I'm not handing it over." She never liked handing off unfinished cases. "And did he have to choose Edwards? He has the worst close rate of all my colleagues."

"Maybe you could suggest someone else."

"Yeah. Me. We both know that if my case is tied to my attack, this man won't stop coming for me. In fact, I'm more motivated than ever to find this guy. Much more motivated than Edwards."

TJ turned into her subdivision and onto her street. Several cars were parked in her driveway. "Looks like your sisters and mother got word about the attack."

"Yeah. I'm sure they did." With most of Leila's sisters in law enforcement, she wasn't surprised they'd descended on her house. They never left out their matriarch either. Lila Kane was known for her wisdom and wit.

They'd want all the details. Ones she couldn't remember. What kind of detective was she, if she couldn't even remember the characteristics of the man who'd attacked her?

Leila stepped from the SUV and walked through the side door into her garage. Before she reached for the interior doorknob she turned back to face TJ, the man she'd almost called her husband.

"Do me a favor. Don't mention the package I received earlier. If this is something other than a one-off attack, we need the official word from the precinct. The last thing I need is Quinn blaming me for initiating a public panic or my family's protective frenzy that will ensue if they think this was a serial killer."

She wasn't sure she should even say the words.

"It isn't over. What other kind of killer marks their victims with a blood pin?"

"I'm hoping for an obsessive fan or someone who wants to scare the homicide detective into not doing her job."

"Understood. Don't worry, I've got your back. Especially since I'm in charge of your protective detail."

She tensed with the revelation. "Quinn put *you* in charge?"

"Said he thought I would be best since I know you so well. Figured I could keep you out of trouble but we both know that's not true."

He was teasing her. Funny how quickly

they fell back into familiar banter. TJ always made the darkness of life seem a bit lighter and she fought the urge to seek any comfort from her ex. Their relationship was over and she couldn't go back to the way things had been. The one large argument they had about her promotion to the homicide unit was only the result of a much deeper problem still unraveling between them. His jealousy over her position had given him the out he had coveted for a long time. She had known he wanted the job ever since his father had been killed in the line of duty. TJ was only sixteen years old at the time of his death.

The title of detective was his dream and she'd taken the one open spot away from him. His accusations of betrayal were understandable but broke their trust on both sides.

She couldn't pass up the only chance she might have to work as a detective. If she were honest, they'd been having issues before she got her promotion. Seemed like that was what forced them to face the reality they were not meant to be together long term.

Leila smiled, turned back to the door and straightened her shoulders, then entered through the mudroom of her home. A flurry of hugs came at her from first her mother, then her four sisters—Dani, Sasha, Holly and Chelsea.

Dani held her the longest. "I'm so sorry, sis. I should've gone with you like I always do."

She pulled back from her twin sister's embrace. "Why? So you could've been hurt too? I'm thankful you had a migraine and couldn't go."

They hugged again then joined the others and TJ.

All their voices quieted and gazes settled on her. They wanted details so they could get to work putting a plan together, but the details in her mind were vague at best. Not even a concrete height or weight. All she remembered was his dark eyes and massive strength. "I think it's safe to say that this wasn't a crime of opportunity," Leila said. "TJ and I believe this was a coordinated attack with the potential that the assailant had been surveilling me."

"And he's still out there, watching you," Dani said, her eyes wide with worry.

"True," TJ said. "But Sergeant Quinn has assigned me to oversee protection detail while the investigative team works to find Leila's attacker. We'll be pulling security footage from the neighbors' home cameras and street cams to see if we can get an ID on him or his vehicle."

Holly filled a glass with water. "It's likely he'll come for her again. Especially if he took the time to watch her."

Leila glanced at her mother. The older woman remained quiet, listening to the entire conversation.

"I agree." TJ sat back. "That does seem to fit with what we know about him. We believe he wasn't only targeting Leila but also—"

"But also—" Leila interrupted in an effort to control the narrative and keep the blood pin quiet. TJ might say too much and worry her sisters more than necessary at this time. "This guy could be tied to the current murder case I'm working. I'm hoping he's just trying to keep me from digging into the investigation."

"We can help with security, TJ," Sasha said. "Dani, Chelsea, Holly and I can stay with her and help out any other patrols that Quinn sets up. I know the precinct is short-staffed right now from underfunding."

"Thanks. We'll take all the help we can get. The main goal is to keep the attacker from getting anywhere near Leila again. I've been assigned to guard her while on the job and if you all can help with the after-hours coverage, then she should be safe until we have him behind bars."

The doorbell rang, interrupting their meeting. TJ glanced at Leila. "Are you expecting company?"

"I wasn't expecting any of this but here we are." She stood and moved to the door with TJ in tow.

"Let me get the door. It's not safe for you to be exposed."

Leila pulled back the side curtain and frowned at him. "It's Dave Masterson. He lives across the street and put in my security alarm. He's a nice guy."

TJ place a hand on the knob and lowered his voice. "Those are the ones that make the best serial killers."

"He's not going to kill me with everyone here and you hovering over me like a bouncer in a club. Plus, the man can't be more than a hundred and eighty pounds and my attacker was closer to two fifty. At least I think he was."

Leila placed her hand over TJ's. His firm grip was warm underneath hers but as soon as she touched his fingers, he pulled away. One way to get him to move.

She opened the door. "Hi, Dave. Come on in."

The man who wasn't much older than her

stepped into the foyer. "I heard about what happened to you. The whole neighborhood is buzzing about it."

"Well, you can see I'm fine."

Dave moved to her security box without hesitation and punched a couple of keys, triggering the screen to come alive. He didn't pay TJ any mind.

"My alarm is fine, Dave."

"Did you not arm it, then? Is that how he got inside?"

"I wasn't home when I was attacked."

"Oh." The man turned toward her again. "Well, that's good. I'm glad you're okay and that your alarm is working properly."

Dave peered around the wall and across the open floor plan, to where all of her sisters were gathered around the table working on a protective detail schedule for her safety. "Looks like you're busy. Let me know if you need anything."

"Will do. Thanks for stopping by."

When he was gone, Leila turned back to TJ. "See. Nothing to worry about."

"That guy likes you."

"He does not. He's got a fiancée and is a concerned neighbor."

"He likes you."

She smacked at his arm. "Stop. He does not."

They returned to the kitchen with a laugh, drawing all her sisters' eyes in their direction. Heat rushed up Leila's neck and into her cheeks. "Don't y'all need to be working?"

They organized work schedules, assigned babysitting duty, pulled social media data on her victim as well as plotted out a timeline for Leila's attack, comparing it to her current case.

All the extra work made Leila more anxious. She loved her family but a part of her worried that she might be putting them in a more dangerous situation. If what TJ mentioned earlier was true and they *were* chasing down a serial killer, then she didn't want them to be in harm's way. She'd never forgive herself if this psychopath went after any of them. But she needed their help to stop this man.

Once the details were all finalized, they gathered their things and headed toward the door. Except Holly. She had first watch with Leila tonight.

Dani leaned toward her ear and interrupted her thoughts. "Can I talk to you in private?"

"Of course." Leila stood and followed her twin sister toward the back hallway and mudroom. She stopped when Dani faced her. "I didn't want to tell you this in front of Mom. She'd worry even more than she already is."

"Okay, what's up?"

Dani shifted her weight to her other foot. "At my PI office three weeks ago, a man came in and hired me to find his wife, Kitty St. Claire. One day when he arrived home from a business trip, she wasn't there. He didn't think much about it at first since she was a busy lady and her gaggle of gossipy friends always kept her—"

"Wait." Leila held up her hand. "Gaggle of gossipy friends?"

"His words, not mine."

"Nice. Okay, continue."

"Anyway, her friends kept her days filled with lunches, gym workouts and spa appointments, but she came home every night. Until she didn't. I figured she was having an affair and ran off with her boyfriend, but the girl was faithful as a golden retriever. My team has no leads to find her and we all know that with every passing moment her life is in more danger."

"Has the husband filed a missing person report?"

"He did not. Something about not trusting the police. So he hired me to work the case.

Said he'd heard about my reputation finding missing persons and hired me on the spot. I encouraged him to file with the police and he refused."

"And no one else has reported her missing to police? Not her friends or family?" Leila leaned against the wall.

"Nothing that I've found."

"That's odd."

"It gets odder. Last night, I came across some street cam footage showing her being abducted during her morning jog like you. Eerily similar to your attack, except the man took her. We've yet to find a body. I was going to the police today until…"

"Until my attack."

"Yeah, and get this. She was taken from Hyacinth Street."

"In this subdivision?"

"Yeah. The wealthy side on the other end. Larger lots, massive homes but still technically a part of Shadow Forest. Apparently, she retired from the military, used the money she got to start a skin care business that exploded into an empire. You've heard of Soho Skin, haven't you?"

"Yeah, I use their face wash and scrub every night."

"Well, you can thank Kitty St. Claire…if we find her."

"You will. You always do."

Her sister shook her head. "What bothers me is her attack was so similar to yours. Makes me sick to think how close you were to not being here."

A glassiness filled her sister's eyes. Leila placed a hand on hers. "But I am *here*. He didn't get me but we also have to make sure he doesn't take anyone else."

"Agreed, but I didn't want to share this info and get rumors started that might increase public panic. After hearing about your current investigation, my case and now your attack, I think we may be looking at a serial killer."

"TJ and I discussed the same theory." Leila leaned back against the wall. "Did she get a red box delivered to her home?"

"I'm not sure, but I can ask. Her husband didn't mention it if she did."

"Ask. My victim and I both had a red box delivered. When I opened mine, it had a blood pin inside. Like the one Dad had. Stacy Green had the same piece sunk into her chest when they found her body off the Blue Ridge Parkway at Wildcat Falls."

"I'll find out and let you know."

"Thanks. If Kitty St. Claire did receive a pin, then we have to tell the precinct so they can develop a task force."

They headed toward the front door and Dani gave her a hug. "I can stay the night and we can work on this, if you want."

Leila released her sister. "That's okay. Holly has first watch and I'm exhausted. I'm headed straight to bed."

"I'm so glad you're okay."

"Me too."

Dani exited and Leila's other sisters filed into the small foyer area to bid their farewell. She hugged each one, giving her mother a little kiss on the cheek. Worry filled the older woman's eyes.

"I don't like this, Leila."

"Neither do I, Mom, but we've got the best homicide unit working this case and we'll catch him. Everyone makes a mistake at some point."

"The pin you asked about earlier. Does it have to do with this?"

"Mom, you know I can't discuss the details with you."

"I know but I used to take comfort in the fact that when you worked homicide cases the killers never seemed to hunt you, but this one is different. Is there more to this case than what you're telling us?"

Her mother always had a way of knowing when she was holding back. "Nothing I can divulge at this time. Once I can provide more details I will."

Lila hugged her neck again. "Let me know if you need more info on your father during his military time." She turned to go, then stopped. "Oh. I forgot to say goodbye to TJ. I'm really thankful he'll be overseeing your protective detail. Must be nice having him around again."

Leila forced a smile. She wasn't sure about that and found herself struggling with his current presence. Now they'd be spending more time together in the future. Talk about awkward.

After the last of her sisters' cars pulled out of the driveway, all except Holly who was staying the night, Leila turned to go back inside but a familiar scent stopped her. She backed up to the door, scanning the area in front of her. There was no one there. At least not that she could see. Another cold wind whipped the smell away from the area but there was no denying it was the same skunky scent from the man who'd attacked her.

He'd been there.

Watching her. Just like Dani said.

* * *

TJ stood in front of Leila's kitchen sink and washed the last of the cups. He'd never imagined he'd be back here doing the same mundane task again. Leila had a dishwasher but never used the thing. Always said she could wash them by hand faster, and since he enjoyed the alone time with her, he'd never complained.

Despite their past history, he'd enjoyed spending time with Leila and her sisters. Being around them, all together, gave him a sense of a loving family that he really didn't have as a child. His mother was nothing like Lila Kane, a warm, wise and strong matriarch who'd shaped her girls into independent women. At the ripe age of seventy-five she still ran their family dairy farm after her husband's death. They were all smart, capable women and understood his law enforcement mind. Not many could relate to the danger officers faced every day to keep communities safe but had no problem judging negative results when split-second, life-altering decisions had to be made.

Footsteps shuffled behind him and he turned with a sudsy cup in hand.

"I wanted to come say my goodbyes but certainly didn't expect you to be in here cleaning up." Lila walked into the room and joined him at the sink. TJ liked that Leila had been named after her mother with the *e* as a slight variation, but the two women shared more familial traits than their name.

"I guess old habits die hard."

"I guess so." She scraped a few scraps from a plate into the trash can and slipped it into the water. "I wanted to thank you for looking out for Leila. I know this arrangement can't be easy, but I admire you for putting your differences aside to keep my daughter safe."

"I'll do my best."

"I know you will." She patted his shoulder. "You're an honorable man and always do a job well."

"I think you and I both know protecting Leila is more than a job for me."

She held his gaze with her soft blue eyes that wrinkled at the corners. "That's why I trust you with my daughter. I know she can be independent, sometimes to her detriment, but you know how to keep her stubbornness in check."

"I don't know about that. Sometimes she's hard to handle."

"I suppose so. She gets that from me, ya know."

"You don't say." He shot her a teasing smile, which she returned.

"You remind me of my late husband. Cool and calm under pressure. We had a rough patch in our relationship about the time when I was pregnant with my twin girls. We were separated for a while. I'm not even sure Leila knows about that time, so might be best not to mention it. With all that said, when love is true, somehow God always has a way of bringing two people back together. Forgiveness is key."

TJ plunged his hand into the soapy water for the next cup. "I'm glad that worked out for you and your husband. That might be where Leila and I differ, though. We can forgive, just not sure we can forget."

"Who said anything about forgetting? If you forget, then you can't remember the pain that keeps us from making the same mistakes again. Forgiveness doesn't have to include forgetting but instead letting go of the debt the other person should pay."

TJ swirled the sponge inside the cup. "I just think our lives are in different places."

"You never know. However, I'll stop harping and tell you that if you need a safe place to stay, you can always bring Leila to the farm. We have plenty of room."

"Thanks. I'll keep that in mind."

She pointed at the cup he was rinsing under the water. "You missed a spot."

The petite woman shuffled from the room and disappeared back toward the foyer. In a few minutes, the front door creaked open and shut, with her mother telling Leila goodbye.

A low rumble echoed from the street. TJ looked out the small window decorated with a ruffled curtain. Nothing out there but the neighborhood cat curled up in one of Leila's outdoor chairs for the night. The echo faded after a few seconds. Probably just a neighbor headed home for the evening.

Forgiveness. He wasn't sure Leila would ever be able to forgive him for their breakup. They'd said some pretty mean things to each other that night and their words caused long-lasting damage.

TJ plunged another cup into the hot, sudsy water, his hand turning red from the temperature. Should've used the dishwasher for all these.

Soft footsteps tapped the floor behind him. He didn't even need to turn to know Leila had entered the room. He'd recognize her footsteps anywhere.

She smiled when he looked at her, picked up a drying towel and wiped one of the glasses he'd placed in the drain. "Thanks for coming tonight. Your insight into all of this was helpful, and with all the questions they had, I was glad to have you there to answer a few. You don't have to stay, though. I can finish these up. I'm sure you'd like to get home too."

He kept washing. "I figured I'd stay."

She leaned her hip against the counter and tilted her head like she used to do when she didn't know if she agreed with his decision. "Here?"

"Yeah."

"You're not going home?"

"Hadn't planned on it." He kept washing, hoping his idea to offer another layer of protection wouldn't turn into an argument.

She placed the glass into the cabinet. "Holly's got first watch. You don't need to stay."

He twisted the sponge down into the next glass and gave it a twist. "There's no way I'm leaving you and your sister alone with a psychopath out there." A few suds flung onto the window screen when he motioned outside. "I can sleep on the couch near the door."

Leila didn't say anything more. Maybe she'd see that having him here wasn't such a bad idea after the attack today. He'd accidentally overheard the conversation between Leila and

Dani also and he didn't feel good about leaving them alone. This was more than a one-off attack. The guy would return.

With two female joggers plus Leila's attack occurring in the last few weeks and the bizarre red box with the blood pin as a connection, this was no doubt the work of a serial killer.

He'd have to tell Sergeant Quinn, even if the precinct liked to keep those details under wraps until they were 100 percent sure.

TJ scrubbed the last glass, rinsed the dish and placed it into the plastic drain before tearing off a paper towel to dry his hands. He took aim and tossed the rolled-up wad into the trash can.

"Score," he said, turning to face her.

Leila was still quiet. Somewhat of a surprise, since he could tell by her body language she was about to launch into an argument. She always pressed her lips together when she was thinking of a way to make her objections. Then again, maybe she was more worried than he realized.

She dried the glass and returned it to the cabinet. "I appreciate the offer of you staying the night, but we'll be fine," she said. "Holly and I are both tired even though I'm sure I won't sleep much. My brain will be working overtime and I don't want to keep you awake since we're scheduled to be at work in six hours."

She walked to the door, lifted his jacket from the hanger and held out the garment. He hesitated, but after seeing the determined look on her face he figured this was not the battle to fight.

TJ kept his gaze on her. "I don't like you being alone. He could come back. He knows where you live. Why not let me stay? I promise not to bother you."

"I'm not alone. Holly's here. I don't want to burden others and we're not together anymore. You've done your work and put together a good security plan. I trust it will work. Besides, Quinn has two guard patrols posted outside. That should be plenty."

Her stubbornness annoyed him. Same old Leila. Too independent to let anyone help. If he was honest with himself, their past relationship had been on the rocks long before she got the detective job over him. She always kept walls up and never fully let him into her life.

"I think this is one of those times when it's okay to burden friends and family. If we can't help in situations like this, then what good are we?"

She placed her hand against his chest, the warmth of her touch radiating through his shirt. "I appreciate the offer and promise that if anything out of the ordinary happens, I'll call. But we both need some rest and I don't think you will get that if you sleep on my hard, lumpy couch. I'll see you in the morning when you pick me up. Besides, he won't come back tonight. Criminals never strike twice on the same day and there has been way too much activity around here for him to be stupid enough to return."

She motioned to her white box on the wall. "And I have Dave's handy-dandy security system. I'll make sure to arm it tonight and no one will get through this door without the cops being notified. I'll be fine."

"If it works."

"Be nice."

Her hand fell away as she pulled the front door open for him to leave. TJ stepped onto the porch and Leila followed. March nights were still cold and he pulled his jacket on, zipping it up before stopping at the top of the steps. "If anything out of the ordinary happens tonight, call me, okay? Don't try to take this killer down all by yourself."

She pressed a palm to her chest. "I promise I'll call."

Bright headlight beams lit up her face, flashing in her blue eyes. TJ turned as an engine roared up the road. He stepped to the bottom of the steps. The back of the vehicle was large and burgundy. "Is that the van?"

The vehicle spun its tires and sped up the hill, disappearing around a corner. TJ's heart dropped into his stomach as adrenaline flooded his veins. It had to be the same van that tried to abduct Leila earlier. How many burgundy vans could there be in Shadow Forest?

He whistled to the patrol car parked in Leila's driveway. The officer sprang into action and gave chase with blue lights flashing. TJ jogged to his SUV and motioned for the second officer to stay with Leila.

"TJ— Wait."

He didn't stop, didn't even look back at her as he reached his car. "Stay with the guard and Holly," he said over his shoulder.

If he wanted to keep this killer from hurting her again, then the last thing she needed was to be involved in this chase. It would be safer for her to stay home. TJ, on the other hand, planned to catch this assailant before the man got away and took the life of another innocent woman.

He peeled out of Leila's driveway, the tires kicking up dirt from the side of her yard as he tore into the street. Up ahead, he could see the patrol car's flashing lights as it closed in on the suspicious van. Other units were already being alerted over the radio to assist and cut off potential escape routes.

TJ's knuckles turned white from his grip on the steering wheel. If this was their guy, if this was the man who had attacked Leila and maybe other women too, he wasn't going to let him get away this time. No matter what it took.

As he approached the intersection, the van made a hard right turn with the patrol car right behind it. TJ followed, the tires screeching in protest. He caught a glimpse of the van's make and model and relayed it over his radio.

"Suspect vehicle is a burgundy Ford Econoline van, license plate, HJR 007. Last seen heading east on Morrison Boulevard."

The chase continued for several more blocks with TJ driving as fast as he dared on the residential streets, trying to catch up to the patrol car. They couldn't let this guy get away. They had to stop him before he struck again.

Up ahead, the van swerved to avoid an oncoming car and the patrol car was forced to hit the brakes, temporarily losing ground. TJ floored it, determined not to let the suspect get any further ahead.

As he blew through the intersection against

the red light, another patrol car joined from a side street, pursuing the van with sirens blaring. Good, backup.

The van plowed through the next red light. TJ punched the gas harder to follow. A white box truck approached from the side street and crossed. TJ slammed on the brakes but he was going too fast.

The front end of his cruiser slammed into the rear quarter panel of the white truck. The impact jarred TJ's body. Metal crunched and shattered glass filled the air. The seat belt cut into his chest and plastic airbags hit his face, full force.

Insistent ringing assaulted his ears and pain throbbed through his head from the collision. He blinked to regain his senses as smoke began wafting up from the crushed hood of his car.

The van fled in the distance, getting further and further away. The other patrol cars still gave chase, but a sinking sensation filled the pit of TJ's stomach. They were losing him and he'd be free to kill again. Or worse, go back for Leila.

He fumbled for the radio mic, his ears still ringing. "10-52. Ambulance needed. I've wrecked into a white truck. Backup still in pursuit of burgundy van."

TJ dropped the mic, threw off his seat belt and shoved open the crumpled door, almost falling onto the pavement. He had to see if the other driver was okay.

A middle-aged man sat dazed behind the wheel of the white truck. TJ rushed over, his flashlight shining into the car. Spilled coffee beans littered the seats and floor. Several boxes were overturned.

"Mackey?" TJ asked, realizing he'd hit the owner of his favorite coffee truck.

"Yeah. I thought I had a green light."

"Are you injured? Does anything hurt?"

Mackey moved around a bit and brushed loose beans from his lap. The scent of coffee permeated the air. "Everything seems fine. Except for my supplies."

"Looks like we spilled the beans."

Mackey shot him a narrowed look and stepped out of the damaged car. "Not funny, man."

"Yeah. Sorry."

"Am I going to get a ticket? I promise I didn't see your lights and had my earbuds in, playing loud music."

"Your light was green and not sure how you didn't see the blue lights, but accidents happen. I should've slowed more when crossing the intersection. We're in pursuit of a suspect."

Mackey motioned in the direction of the other cop cars, now disappeared from their site. "The burgundy van?"

"You know it?"

His friend walked around to the back of his box truck and opened the doors. Another box of coffee beans spilled onto the road. "Great." He brushed them aside and straightened the remaining boxes. "I don't know the driver but I've seen that van in our neighborhood some. Especially lately."

Another patrol car pulled up beside them. "Need a lift?"

Sergeant Quinn sat in the driver's seat.

"Yeah. Give me a minute." TJ turned back to Mackey. "A couple of patrol units will be here with the paramedics. Get checked out, make sure you're okay and then give a statement to the officers about the accident and the van. Okay?"

Mackey still seemed a bit confused by all the commotion but nodded in agreement. "And my supplies?"

"We'll work the details out."

TJ hopped inside the patrol car with his sergeant.

"He okay?" his superior asked.

"Seems to be. I hit him pretty hard, though. Paramedics are going to check him out."

The radio crackled with another update from the pursuing officers. "Suspect vehicle just crashed through a roadblock and is heading west toward the Blue Ridge Parkway entrance."

"I know a shortcut." Sergeant Quinn took a hard left and ran a back highway that spit them out just above the entrance. The burgundy van was nowhere in sight but couldn't be far as patrol cars blew past them and into a sharp curve. Tires screeched and sirens blared.

TJ and Quinn followed, rounding the curve to find the other officers all stopped or pulling to the side of the road. Bright headlights from one of the vehicles glared into the woods, highlighting the van.

The front end was smashed into a rocky embankment. Debris littered the road in all directions but the driver's-side door was open.

Two more patrol cars skidded to a stop behind Quinn and TJ. Officers swarmed from their cars with weapons drawn and took cover behind their vehicles.

"Police, put your hands up," one of them said.

There was no movement from inside the van. TJ took the lead, his own gun aimed at the driver's door and adrenaline coursing through his body. Was this finally it? Had they caught the man who'd attacked Leila?

TJ remained close to the side of the van and used the toe of his shoe to push the bent driver's door further open. Shattered glass rained to the ground. The metal creaked, but when TJ pivoted into place, the seat was empty, with no sign of the suspect.

"Clear," he said, instant defeat fueling his frustration.

Quinn stepped up beside him. "How did he get out without us seeing?"

"No idea." TJ swept the interior of the van with his flashlight. "But he can't be far."

No one was inside, but there were clear signs of a struggle—ripped fabric, smeared blood and, most chilling of all, strands of blond hair stuck in the edges of the back window.

A new wave of dread crashed over him. The attacker hadn't just been fleeing from Leila's home tonight. The killer had another victim.

THREE

After TJ left without her, Leila ran back inside her house to grab her weapon and keys. She got that he was trying to protect her, but she was a cop. One with the rank of detective. No one was going to keep her locked up like a princess in a tower. He wasn't her knight in shining armor on his white horse. Far from it, actually.

Her hands trembled from the adrenaline rush as she fumbled with her gun, but the weight of it was comforting in her grip. She slammed a loaded magazine into her weapon as Holly descended the stairs and moved past her, standing in front of the door to peer out the window.

"What's going on? I heard sirens." Her sister turned and let her gaze fall to the keys in Leila's hand. Her eyes widened with concern. "Don't think you are going anywhere. At least not until you tell me what's going on."

Leila took a deep breath, trying to calm

her pounding heart. "The same van from earlier raced past the house. TJ left to chase him down. That was his siren you heard when he ran off and left me. Now, can you move so I can go get the man who tried to kill me?"

Holly's face paled. "Not gonna happen."

Leila held her sister's determined stare for a moment. Holly was a black belt in jiujitsu, and even though Leila was also trained, she knew there was no beating Holly. She'd been up against her sister before.

"Come on, Holly. Don't be like this."

"Like what? Your older sister who loves you? Besides, I'm not going to be the one who has to answer to Mom when you get yourself killed by chasing down the man who wants you dead. You're staying here tonight. Let TJ and the officers do their job."

"This is my job too. I'm the detective on the case." Leila's voice rose, her patience wearing thin.

"Which is why the killer wants you dead." Holly's words hung in the air, heavy with worry.

"You really aren't going to let me go?"

Her sister locked the dead bolt with a decisive click. "Nope."

Realizing she wasn't going to win this battle, Leila placed her gun on the entry table, moved into the living room and dropped to the sofa. "I still can't believe he left me behind. Infuriating man."

Holly took a seat beside her, her presence both comforting and frustrating. "He's just trying to do his job and keep you safe. Don't be too hard on him."

"He might need me there."

"He's got plenty of help and you know it. The entire team will be backing him up. For once in your life why not stick to the plan?" Holly motioned toward the window. "The killer is out there and would love to get you separated from your guards, then he'll have the perfect opportunity to finish what he started."

Leila stared at her sister for a moment, hating when Holly was right. She rested her head back on the cushion and silently counted the rotations of the ceiling fan. Too much time had passed for her to be able to catch the man anyway. She'd have to miss the one opportunity to bring a serial killer to justice. The thought frustrated her but at least he'd be behind bars.

"Fine," she said.

"Good. Let your fellow cops hunt this guy for you. They are a top-notch unit and can keep you safe."

"I get it. I do. And if it were one of you I'd

be saying the exact same thing, but this guy is tied to my current case. I should be there when they arrest him."

"You'll have plenty of time with him once they bring him in. This is their moment. You'll have yours. Besides, I'd rather you be alive than in a body bag."

Holly never sugarcoated the truth but had a way of persuading people to think logically in the midst of danger. The rest of the Kane sisters were a bit more impulsive but not Holly. Her oldest sister saw the big picture better than anyone in the state, making her a sought-after forensic profiler.

"You're right. I just hate not being a part of things." Leila's shoulders slumped in defeat.

"I'll make you some chamomile tea. Maybe that will help calm you."

Another trait Holly had picked up from their mother. Anytime one of her girls or friends was feeling bad, Lila Kane made a cup of tea.

Holly disappeared around the corner, taking with her Leila's keys and weapon. Her sister was no dummy. The thought had crossed Leila's mind to sneak out, but with her keys in her sister's possession, there really wasn't a good way.

Like tea was going to help. Leila wanted

to be right in the action, not sitting inside her home like a prisoner. She pulled a small pillow to her chest and closed her eyes, fighting the wave of emotions triggering tears. She swiped a finger at the corner. The last thing she needed was her sister to see her crying. She'd really hover over her then.

A loud clang echoed from the kitchen. Leila sat bolt upright, her heart pounding. She stayed still, waiting for Holly's explanation, but none came. She strained to hear any other noises. Maybe Holly had dropped the teakettle.

"Holly? You okay?"

"I'm fine," Holly's voice sounded strained. "Just finishing up your green tea."

Confusion prompted her to stand and move toward the kitchen. "You know I don't like green tea. I thought you were making chamo—"

She rounded the corner and froze. The glint of a knife blade flashed into view, pressed against Holly's throat. Leila's breath caught in her chest and every nerve tightened inside her body.

Holly stood rigid, her face drained of color, eyes wide with fear. The killer from earlier loomed behind her sister, the details of his face covered with the same black hoodie and scarf.

"Don't hurt my sister. I'll go with you," Leila

said, holding up her palms, her voice trembling despite her best efforts to stay calm.

Holly shifted her weight ever so slightly against her captor's hold, but he didn't budge. His grip was as steely as it had been when he'd grabbed Leila that morning. Holly's gaze flickered toward the stool a few feet away where Leila's loaded gun sat.

Understanding her sister's unspoken message, Leila inched forward as if to surrender. "Let her go and I'll go with you. You don't want her. You want me, though I'm not sure why you do."

"That's selfless of you," he said.

A rasp filled his voice, deep and low, providing a toughness reserved for mafia movies. Why would he care if she was being selfless? Of course, she'd give her life for any one of her sisters without a second thought. Wouldn't most people?

"Leila." Holly's voice trembled. "Don't go with him."

In a blur of motion, the killer raised the knife's wooden handle and brought it crashing down against Holly's temple. Her sister crumpled to the floor with a sickening thud.

Leila's training kicked in, overriding her shock. She lunged for the gun, her fingers closing around the grip as she brought it up and fired. But the killer had already disappeared into the shadowy hallway, the bullet embedding itself harmlessly into the sheetrock wall.

Heart racing, Leila rushed to Holly's side. Her fingers found a pulse, strong and steady, though a nasty knot was already forming on her sister's head from the blow.

"I'll help you," Holly said as she roused and tried to sit up but swayed from the effort. She lowered herself back down, her face pale. "Give me just a minute."

"Stay here." Leila pulled out her phone and pressed it into Holly's shaking hand. "Call 911. I'm going after him."

"Don't." Holly grabbed Leila's wrist with surprising strength. "He'll kill you, Leila. He wants you isolated and alone."

"I've got my gun and the patrol guard is outside. Text him for backup." Leila pried her arm from her sister's tight grip. "I'll be fine." She had to stop this maniac before he hurt anyone else.

A dull thump echoed from down the hallway, spurring Leila into action. The drive-by earlier had just been a distraction to separate her from TJ. Where was the guard who was posted outside? With her shot fired, she figured he'd be inside by now. She prayed her attacker didn't harm him.

One thing Holly was right about—he wanted her vulnerable and unprotected. Well, she planned to give him exactly that.

She was a cop first and worked best when someone threatened her family or her. After checking each room, Leila made her way down the corridor—guest bath, clear; spare bedroom, clear; office, clear. The basement door hung ajar at the end of the hall. Of course, he'd be drawn to the basement's maze of cluttered spaces and dark corners.

Leila swallowed hard, mustering her courage. This was it—the only way to end this game. She gripped her gun tighter, nudged the door open with her foot and descended the creaky wooden stairs.

When she reached the bottom, she paused. Something shuffled behind her as if an old box had been knocked aside. He was down here.

The single, bare bulb didn't provide much light, casting deep shadows in every direction. Leila's heart pounded with the rhythm of her own labored breath as she crept forward, scanning each dimly lit recess for any sign of movement.

The dank, musty air suffocated her, but she

kept inching forward, careful to clear every spot—each one a potential ambush point—behind the towering stacks of storage boxes, clustered heaps of discarded furniture and all the unlighted alcoves.

She pivoted and aimed her weapon behind her father's old armoire. Nothing.

The light shifted behind her. With a quick pivot, she turned, weapon raised. The pull-string attached to the bulb swayed and the basement door was open.

She moved toward the exit, hoping to get his direction, but when she stepped into the door-frame the streetlamp highlighted her silhouette, revealing her location. A rookie mistake.

He burst from the darkness, knocked her gun from her hand and pulled her body back into the basement, toward the stairs.

Leila struggled against his iron grip, her training kicking in as she threw her elbows and tried to break free. But he was stronger, his arm like a vise around her chest as he dragged her deeper into the basement.

"Stop."

"Not a chance, Detective Kane. You're my next paycheck."

Leila's mind raced. His next paycheck? She

tried to piece together the clues, but escaping the physical threat was her first priority.

With the backyard enclosed by a locked iron fence, he forced her back up the stairs. His van must be parked on the street and backup units would have him surrounded if her sister had called for help.

He shoved her into the kitchen where Holly was still on the floor. Unmoving.

Panic surged through Leila at her sister's still form. She struggled against her captor, desperate to reach her.

"Holly." Leila searched for any sign of life. If she had a bleed or a skull fracture then she needed a hospital.

The killer tightened his grip, pulling Leila toward the front door. "She's not your concern anymore, Detective. We have places to be."

Leila's mind raced. She had to help Holly and couldn't let this man take her away. With a sudden burst of energy, she stomped hard on his instep and threw an elbow into his ribs.

The killer grunted in pain, his grip loosening just enough for Leila to break free. She spun around with a round kick, her foot connecting with his jaw. He staggered back, giving her the opening she needed.

Leila darted back into the kitchen, her eyes

scanning for any weapon. She spotted Holly's gun on the counter and dove for it, her fingers closing around the grip just as the killer recovered and lunged at her.

He wrestled the gun away, knocked her into a chair and stood over her. Their eyes locked for a moment, a silent standoff as his finger hovered over the trigger.

"Who hired you?" she said, as she slid the chair back against a wall.

The killer's eyes narrowed but he didn't respond.

"Give me a name." She tried again, while standing slowly, hands raised.

"Not gonna happen."

A distant siren echoed outside. She followed his gaze out the sliding glass door then back to her sister as he took a step in Holly's direction.

"Stay away from her."

He scooped up the cell phone Leila had given Holly and turned the screen for her to view. "Looks like she never finished the call and she's going to need some help." He held his thumb over the number. "Come with me and I'll hit the call button."

If she went with him, she'd seal her own fate, but if she didn't, Holly might die. There was no other option. He had her weapon and the only lifeline to any assistance.

"Hit Call and I'll come with you."

"Once we're in the van."

She walked within reach as he placed the phone on the island and pressed the key. He held her in a strong grip, but if she played the moment well, she'd be able to escape soon. At least Holly would get the help she needed.

After securing the wreck and crime scene, TJ steered another patrol car toward Leila's house. The time was after midnight, and he was sure she'd be asleep by now, but he had to make certain she and her sister were both okay. After what he'd just witnessed, there was no way he'd leave her alone tonight, no matter her objections.

He turned into the entrance of the neighborhood and stopped at the gatehouse. Pete Bell, the security guard from this morning, stood inside, his cart parked to the left. TJ rolled down his window as the man stepped from the booth and leaned forward. "Hey, you're the officer from this morning. How's Leila doing?"

"A little shaken up, but she'll be fine," TJ replied with caution. He didn't want to give out too many details about Leila's attack or the fact their suspect was still out there, abducting women. "We're still looking for the driver of the burgundy van. You haven't seen him or anyone suspicious in the subdivision tonight, have you?"

The guard shook his head. "I'm only halfway through my shift but I haven't seen anything worrisome, unless you count Mr. Winters walking to his mailbox in his bathrobe. However, I was just getting ready to make my rounds again. Do you want to ride along?"

"Not tonight," TJ said, handing him a card. "But give me a call if you see anything suspicious, okay?"

"Will do. I'll keep a lookout for anyone who shouldn't be here."

"My number's on the back."

The man flipped his card over. "What about Kitty St. Claire? Did y'all ever find her?"

"No new updates yet," TJ said. "You know about her?"

"Word travels fast in this neighborhood."

"What do you know?"

"She lives over on Hyacinth Street. Went jogging the other morning and never came home. Husband reported her missing. Attractive woman. I sure hope she's not mixed up in all this."

"In all of what?" The fact the man brought up Kitty St. Claire on his own raised a red flag. TJ played curious to see how much information the man would divulge.

"I listen to the police scanners, and our whole security team was debriefed about the two female joggers. All from our neighborhood. We're on high alert."

"High alert? How many people are on your security team?"

"Five right now, but I think they are planning to add two more. This is a very large subdivision and the residents aren't happy. Rumors are swirling of a lawsuit against the HOA board if they don't put more of their dues toward security. The ladies that live here are scared and their husbands are demanding a new plan of action or they're going to oust the president."

"And who might that be?" TJ wasn't sure if any of this information would help with the case but they had no leads, so it couldn't hurt.

"Dave Masterson."

TJ sat up a bit straighter. He was the same man who installed Leila's alarm. "The security guy? Installs alarms?"

"Yeah. That's him. Super nice man. Lives across the street from Leila."

Static sounded on Pete's radio, followed by a woman's voice. "Pete, Ms. Clayton's complaining about the neighbor's noise level again. Can you go check things out?"

"10-4." Pete released his mic key. "Gotta run. Duty calls."

Before the guard could leave, TJ asked, "Just curious. Do you live in the neighborhood?"

"Nah. I live in Shadow Estates."

TJ let out a low whistle. "That's high dollar. What did you do? Win the lottery and decide to moonlight as a security guard to keep the boredom away?"

Pete's face fell. "Not exactly. After my dad died, I moved back in with my mom to help take care of her. She's got dementia."

"Oh. Sorry to hear that," TJ said, feeling a twinge of guilt for his assumption.

"It is what it is." Pete gave him a quick nod. "I need to go. We're good?"

"Yeah." TJ watched him head down the hill in his cart and around the corner. Something about the man nagged at his gut, but he couldn't put his finger on what. He seemed harmless enough and had helped Leila in her time of need, but TJ had learned to be thorough and careful. Most serial killers seemed like nice guys to their neighbors. Some were even deacons in their churches. He never understood how one person could live two opposing lives like that. Although someone who strangled the life out of innocent victims didn't dwell on the how.

TJ turned down another side street back to the main route through the subdivision and steered toward Leila's home. He'd never be able to rest if he wasn't nearby with everything that had happened. She was right about most serial killers not striking twice in one day. They wanted to regroup and plan another attack, but he'd never forgive himself if something happened to her or Holly and he wasn't there.

He could always sleep in his SUV. Leila didn't have to know. He could pull into her driveway late and cut the lights. He'd done that before on stakeouts. Not the most comfortable, but he'd be okay. His phone buzzed, and Sergeant Quinn's name flashed on the screen.

"A couple of hikers found another woman's body," Quinn said without preamble. "Lori McCoy. Taken from the same neighborhood and strangled, tying her to the other victims. We're gonna have to move Leila to a safer location. This guy just keeps grabbing women and I don't want him finding her."

TJ gripped his steering wheel tighter. "Was this victim taken while jogging too?"

"Yeah. We have street cam footage of her abduction off Juniper Street. And she has the pin."

"A third victim," TJ said. "That's not good."

"So, you heard about Kitty St. Claire? We haven't found her yet either but I'm guessing it's only a matter of time."

"Most likely." TJ sat up straighter in his seat, his heart racing. "Where'd you find this one?"

"Off the Blue Ridge Parkway, near Sliding Rock. He dumped his first victim, Stacy Greene, within a couple of miles of this lady. Both near rivers. I need you up here to help secure the scene. See if there's anything that matches what Leila told you about her attack."

"On my way."

TJ's mind shifted gears. Instead of heading back to Leila's tonight, he'd try to find out more about the victim. Perhaps he and Leila could build on the profile of who this man might be by learning more about the women he took. She'd be okay for a few hours. Besides, she had Holly and the guard there to protect her. What could go wrong?

"Where am I headed again?" TJ asked, already turning the car around.

"About half a mile from the Sliding Rock

parking area," Quinn hesitated. "On second thought, bring Leila. She'll be able to know more than you if anything matches what happened to her. I want her to talk to the medical examiner to compare notes about Stacy, this victim, and Kitty St. Clair's case."

"I'll swing by and pick her up." TJ turned down another side street, backtracking. "By the way, I have a few thoughts about this guy. Especially now that we have connected cases with multiple bodies."

"Yeah. But let's not talk about it over the phone. Wait until you get here."

TJ ended the call and continued to Leila's house. The day had been rough and he hated to wake her up, but if Quinn wanted her there, then so be it. She was probably used to the interruptions since she worked as a detective now. Homicides never respected a good night's sleep.

He tried her number, but there was no answer. He tried again. Straight to voice mail. Most detectives kept their phones on 24/7. At least his father had. He still remembered his last call to a crime scene. TJ had been sixteen, and his father had to leave his football game early. TJ had scored the winning touchdown at almost the exact time his father was shot while on duty.

The memory sent a chill down his spine as he pulled into Leila's drive. Several of the lights were off in the front. He rang the doorbell, but after a few minutes with no answer, TJ trudged around back through the grass. The kitchen light over the sink was still on and cast a glow across her backyard. He peered through the sliding glass door and raised his hand to knock but stopped when he heard loud voices.

"Why did you tell them it was a false alarm?" Leila said, struggling against a man's grip. "I told you I'd go with you if you completed the 911 call."

The basement door was open, and the man moved her into a headlock. "I lied."

She fought against him, dropped to the ground out of his grasp and knocked the gun to the floor. With a swift kick, she swiped his knee with her booted heel.

TJ jerked on the handle, but the door wouldn't move. Locked. He fought to bounce it off track or even break the glass. Anything to help her.

The man wrapped his hands around Leila's throat and lifted her to her feet. She clawed his arms, but her fight was fading. If TJ didn't act fast, he'd witness Leila's murder. He pulled out his weapon, aimed at the glass and prayed he didn't hit her with a stray shot.

The glass shattered with an ear-splitting crack. He didn't wait for the shards to settle before he climbed through, ignoring the cuts on his hands and arms.

"Police. Let her go." TJ kept his gun aimed at the attacker.

The man's eyes widened in surprise, but he didn't release Leila. Instead, he pulled her closer, creating a human shield. "Back off, cop. Or I'll snap her neck."

TJ's mind raced. He couldn't get a clean shot without risking Leila's life. "Let her go, and we can talk about this," he said, trying to keep his voice steady. "You don't want to add cop-killing to your charges."

"You think I care about charges? I'm taking her with me."

Leila's eyes met TJ's. She was fading fast, but she wasn't giving up. In a sudden move, she threw her head back, connecting with the attacker's nose. He howled in pain, his grip loosening just enough for Leila to slip free.

TJ didn't hesitate. As soon as Leila was clear, he fired twice. The attacker stumbled backward, crashed into the kitchen counter and slid to the floor in a daze.

He cuffed his hands, removed his mask with no recognition and checked the assailant for a pulse. Strong. That didn't make sense. He'd sunk two bullets into the guy's chest but there was no blood. TJ ripped open the man's shirt—a bulletproof vest. Of course. His detainee stirred and opened his eyes.

"You're under arrest." He mirandized him and then moved back to Leila's side. "Are you okay?"

She gasped for air and nodded toward her sister. "Holly."

He moved to her sister's side and checked for a pulse. "She's alive. Weak but alive."

Leila crawled across the floor and took her sister's hand while he called for backup and ambulances, rattling off their location like he'd lived here all his life. He almost did but that was no longer an option. He ended the call and sat on the floor next to the two sisters. "She's going to be okay and we got the killer. This is over."

Leila shook her head. "This is far from over. We might've stopped that guy but there will be more."

"What do you mean?"

"Someone hired him. I was his 'paycheck' he was sent to collect. He's not our killer, he's only the front man who abducts the women and I was next on his list. It would be nice to know who sent him."

"Then let's ask."

TJ stood and walked around the island to where he had secured the assailant. His silver handcuffs were on the floor, open. The basement door was ajar.

TJ pulled his weapon and descended the steps then out into the fenced in back yard but there was no sign of Leila's attacker. He must've climbed the fence and vanished into the back woods adjacent to her house. TJ moved to the gate and peered into the side driveway, spotting an officer on the ground. He rushed to his side, pressed two fingers to the officer's neck. Nothing. The one guard he'd left behind to protect Leila was dead. Shot in the head.

With a press of his radio button, TJ made the announcement. He should've sent backup to her house before he instigated the chase.

Quinn was right. They needed to move Leila to a new location. Tonight, before someone else got killed on his watch.

FOUR

Leila gripped her sister's hand, her eyes fixed on Holly's motionless form. The room was silent except for the soft ticking of the clock on the wall, each second stretching into an eternity. She pressed two fingers against Holly's neck once more, feeling for any sign of life. A faint pulse but at least she had one. Her sister's skin was warm and clammy, all color drained from her face. TJ footsteps entered the room behind her.

"What's taking them so long?" Leila kept her focus on her sister. "Her pulse is getting weaker. She could have a skull fracture."

He paced to the window again. "They're five minutes out. Are you okay?"

Leila nodded her head. "I'm fine. I just need to take care of her." She patted Holly's cheeks gently, willing her to regain consciousness. "Come on, Holly, please wake up."

TJ rummaged around behind her and knelt to the floor with a bottle of ammonia. Without hesitation, he grabbed one of Leila's dish towels from a nearby hanger and dampened the fabric with the pungent liquid.

He'd moved around her kitchen with ease, like he'd never left. Part of her was impressed by his willingness to help her sister, while a twinge of sadness reminded her she missed him in her home. She pushed the thought aside, focusing on the task at hand.

TJ handed her the towel, and she placed it under Holly's nose. For a moment, nothing happened. Then, Holly's face scrunched up, her lifeless expression transforming as she turned away from the strong smell.

"I'm right here, Holly." Leila kept her voice soft in case her sister's injury had induced a migraine. "Can you see me? Do you have any pain?"

Holly's voice came out weak and raspy. "Only from the tight squeeze you have on my arm."

Relief washed the tension from Leila and she loosened her grip. "Don't move. The intruder struck your head, and you're bleeding."

But Holly, stubborn as ever, ignored the warning. She pressed herself into a sitting position, leaning her back against the island cabinets for support. "Got another towel? That one stinks."

A small smile tugged at Leila's lips as TJ retrieved another towel. "Sounds like you're going to be just fine."

"Put some ice in it too," Holly said, wincing. "I've got a pretty good migraine."

"I'm so sorry." Leila blinked back the tears that threatened to spill. "This was my worst fear. I never wanted you to get hurt because of me." She surrendered the cold pack to Holly's grasp, watching as her sister pressed it against her head. "And that's exactly what happened. I shouldn't have dragged you all into this."

"Don't be silly. You didn't drag us. We pushed our way in, and we aren't going anywhere. You'd do the exact same thing if it were one of us being targeted."

Her sister was right. There was no way she'd stand idly by while one of her sisters was assaulted. She'd never leave them unprotected if they were in her shoes. The Kane sisters were a tight-knit group, with years of experience in law enforcement between them. But despite all that experience, Leila hadn't seen this attack coming. She'd figured the man disappeared after his first attempt and never expected him to come back for a second attempt in less than twenty-four hours.

"So that was our guy," Holly said, removing the ice from her head for a moment.

TJ nodded. "And he's struck again. I don't think he'll stop coming for Leila as long as she's here."

"I agree. It might be time to move her to a safer location," Holly said. "Somewhere that's easier to guard and out of this neighborhood."

Leila held up her hand. "Hello. I'm right here and can decide for myself."

"Quinn agrees. He wants to move you tonight," TJ said.

She didn't want to leave, but if her sergeant forced her, then there was no other choice. "When did you talk to him?"

"Before I came here. They found another body. Lori McCoy. Do you know her?"

Leila shook her head and he continued.

"She was taken from Juniper Street while on her morning run. They have street cam footage of her abduction apparently. I haven't seen it yet."

"Where'd they find her?" Leila asked.

TJ swallowed. "Off the Blue Ridge Parkway near Sliding Rock. Strangled. Like the others. With an aviation pin."

Holly's face darkened and she tried to stand. "Were all the victims marked with the same pin?"

"Yeah." Leila helped her sister to her feet. "He must pin them before he kills them. It's called blood pinning—a military tradition or initiation somewhat frowned upon but still performed by certain groups."

Holly hugged her sister. "Well, at least he didn't put one on you."

Leila glanced at TJ, a silent exchange passing between them. Holly noticed the look and her forehead creased with concern. "Did you get pinned too?"

"Not exactly. One of the pins was delivered to me after the attack."

"After? That's weird," Holly said. "Most serial killers that use trinkets to mark their victims are quite methodical and stick to their MO."

"I guess I didn't give him an opportunity," Leila said. "I fought back, and he ran out of time."

Holly took a seat in a chair. "The question is, why is he tagging his victims with a blood pin? Was he a paratrooper in the army or part of another branch of military?"

"The most common are army parachutists."

TJ grabbed the first aid kit from her cabinet and handed it to Leila. "Might want to clean her cut. Add a few butterfly bandages."

"Thanks." Leila took a seat next to her sister and opened the kit. "Maybe he's military and wants me to know that."

Holly closed her eyes when Leila applied the betadine. "Or maybe he hates the military or war, and the victims are tied to those efforts somehow."

"A person who hates war but doesn't mind murdering women? He certainly doesn't have an issue with violence." Leila swirled the cleaner around the outside of the cut and then over the surface. Her sister flinched. "That seems a little counterintuitive, even for a madman."

"Not in his mind," Holly said. "Hand me a napkin and pen."

"Let me get the bandages on first." Leila peeled the covering off the adhesive and pulled the cut closed as much as possible. Then she leaned across the table, grabbed a napkin and pen from the center tray.

Holly took the items from her. "If the victims, including you, are affiliated with the military or law enforcement in any way, it could be a trigger for him." Holly's pen flew across the napkin as she spoke. "Maybe he served alongside the victims or someone they loved. Could be a colleague or friend. Many serial killers live normal lives, work and interact with the community until they kill." She motioned across the table. "Hand me another pen. This one died."

Leila's sister mapped out the different locations of the abductions. All from her neighborhood, but a pattern began to emerge. Her sister placed a circle by each location. "One body, Stacy Green, from the east of the neighborhood at Peony Street. Leila's attack was also on the east but more central and Lori McCoy was taken from Juniper Street on the west side of the development."

Leila pointed to Hyacinth Street. "That leaves Kitty St. Clair to the north."

Despite the fact that all these women were being taken from the same neighborhood, Leila still wasn't sure how they'd ever find the man. With thousands of houses across hundreds of acres of property, the task seemed daunting. Did he live nearby or, worse, in the same neighborhood that he used as his personal hunting ground?

"What did the first victim do for a living?" Holly asked, her pen poised over the napkin.

"Stacy Greene was a prosecutor for the state," Leila said.

"And the other one?"

"Kitty St. Claire was a nurse. No connection to the military."

TJ opened an email on his phone and read the details. "Says here Lori McCoy was a high school math teacher which doesn't tie any of their careers together."

"Sounds like he's acting out some kind of revenge. Both victims are in their early thirties, and beautiful. He has a type," Leila said.

"True," Holly agreed. "We just need to find out the connection."

"Still doesn't tell us why he puts a blood pin on them." Leila placed a hand over the area on her chest where the victim's marks lived.

Holly stopped drawing and looked up at her sister. "Can I see the one he sent you?"

"Investigators took it to evidence earlier but I have images." Leila pulled her phone from her pocket, found the pictures and handed the device to her sister.

Holly scrolled through the photos, enlarging some with her fingers. "There are dozens of companies that make pins like this. It's going to be hard to track down the manufacturer, but he's trying to send a message with this pin."

"Let's just hope we can figure out what he wants to say before he strikes again. Maybe he'll lose interest since he wasn't able to pin me."

"Or it'll make him more determined." Holly closed the screen and handed the phone back to Leila. "He'll keep trying until he figures out a way to get the pin on you, or he'll move on to someone else."

"That's not good," TJ said.

Holly nodded. "An understatement, for sure. Dad definitely has a pin like this. I've looked at it multiple times at Mom's house."

Leila placed the phone on the table, her mind racing. "Me too. You don't think he took it from—"

"Nah." Holly waved a hand in the air. "This one's a little different than Dad's."

A knock on the door interrupted their conversation. Leila glanced at her door cam. "Paramedics are here." She stood and let them inside, trying not to obsess over her sister's assessment of their killer.

As she opened the door, Leila's mind whirled with possibilities. She didn't want the killer to target her sisters just to get at her. Maybe it was time to move to a safer location—a place this psychopath would never find her.

TJ had a cabin in the mountains they used to go to for day trips. They had often discussed how they'd expand it and one day retire there, making it a great place for their grandchildren to visit. Now that they were no longer together, she wasn't sure he'd let her back into his sanctuary, but anything was worth a try. Especially if relocating kept her sisters safe.

As the paramedics entered and began examining Holly, Leila caught TJ's eye. He forced a small smile but concern deepened the lines in his face. For a moment, she allowed herself to remember the connection they'd once shared. Despite their broken relationship, she knew he still cared about her safety.

She moved over to where he stood. "I need to ask you something."

"Sure. What's up?"

Leila took a deep breath, steeling herself for the request. "Your cabin in the mountains… I know it's a lot to ask, but do you think I could stay there for a while? Just until we figure this out?"

TJ hesitated at first but then nodded. She tried not to read more into his pause. "Of course. It's secluded, fully stocked and hard to find if you don't know where to look. It might be the perfect place for you to lie low."

"Thanks."

"On one condition of course."

"And what's that?"

"That I go with you."

"I don't think that's a good idea."

"Why not? I'm assigned as your protective officer. Quinn will never let you go alone."

"Because we used to…" Her words trailed. They'd never discussed their past relationship. She wasn't sure she should bring it up now.

TJ crossed his arms over his chest and leaned a shoulder against the kitchen wall. "We used to date, Leila. A lot of people have relationships that don't work out. They're still friends. Staying in my cabin together is not going to put us on some kind of path to reconciliation but it might save your life."

She wasn't sure what to say or how to feel about his revelation. His tone seemed so nonchalant, like staying with her in the cabin where they'd spent many days together didn't mean anything to him. "Apparently you've given this some thought."

He shrugged his shoulders. "Not really. Just makes sense, that's all."

TJ straightened and helped the paramedics push Holly's stretcher out the door as easily as he'd agreed to the cabin plan. Maybe she was overthinking this. She often read more into situations than was there. Maybe they could spend time at the cabin together as professionals. If staying with her didn't bother TJ, then why was she worried?

Instead, she made a mental note to pack, inform her superiors and activate the security system at her house. But for now, she allowed herself a moment of cautious optimism.

Leila walked out to the ambulance to give her sister one last goodbye. Holly managed a weak smile. "Be careful, Lei. Don't let him win."

"I won't. I always was a sore loser."

As she watched the ambulance pull away, Leila turned back toward the house. "After I pack, we can go," she said as she walked past TJ.

"Don't need to pack much. Most of your stuff is still in your bedroom." His revelation stopped her in her tracks. She turned and faced him. "You didn't get rid of my clothes?"

He took her porch steps two at a time and opened the front door of her home. "They're yours. Wasn't my place to get rid of them."

"I just figured you would've wanted them out of your way."

"To be honest, I've not been back."

"Since we broke up?"

"I've been busy."

"But you said the home was stocked."

"Had a friend stay there recently. He made sure to refill the pantry before he left."

She stared at him for a moment longer than comfort allowed.

"But this will be good," he said, quickly recovering. "You can pack up everything while you're there and move it back home when this is over."

With a nod of agreement, Leila excused herself to her bedroom. She grabbed her weekend bag from her closet and sank to her bed. This battle was far from over. If only she knew which battle she was fighting—the one for her life or the one for her heart.

A 1980s Chevy truck rumbled into TJ's drive after dark as he waited inside his small brick rental home for Leila to arrive. She stepped from the driver's side door and walked up his sidewalk. TJ opened the door and let her inside.

"You ready?" she asked.

"Just need to grab my bag." He walked over to the bench near the mudroom. "Where'd you get the truck?"

"It was my dad's. Mom keeps it in the barn and uses it as her farm truck. I thought it might blend in a little better at your mountain cabin instead of the standard cop car."

He grabbed an extra phone charge from the drawer and a battery pack, stuffing them in his bag. Truth was he dreaded going to the cabin with her where so many memories lingered, but how could he refuse when her life was in danger? He didn't want her to be harmed and his cabin was a great option even if it was the last place on earth he wanted to be with her. But Sergeant Quinn's orders were clear: Leila needed protection, and TJ's isolated retreat was the safest option. The place that had once been their sanctuary was now a reluctant refuge.

He lifted the strap to his shoulder. "Let's go."

They exited the house and TJ climbed into the passenger side tossing his bag into the floorboard. "You sure this thing will make the whole trip?"

Leila shoved the key into the ignition and fired the motor right up. "She runs like a champ."

She pulled onto the highway—four lanes of winding asphalt descending down a steep incline to their exit where they'd climb back up a two-lane treacherous road to their safe haven.

A few other late-night drivers passed by but mostly long haulers coasted the highway with them.

"This weather is getting worse." Leila leaned forward and triggered her wipers to clear the moisture from the glass.

Sleet spattered the hood of the truck and flurries blustered around them.

"Just go slow. We should be fine." TJ cracked a window for some fresh air despite the cold temperatures outside. They'd made countless drives to the cabin before, full of laughter and excitement of being alone together. Now silence reigned, broken only by the rumble of passing trucks, staccato of ice pellets on the roof and the hum of tires against the asphalt. If only he could wipe away all the memories of happier times—weekend getaways, lazy mornings and long hikes through the surrounding wilderness—the same way the wiper cleared the windshield. Wouldn't that be nice.

He sensed Leila's discomfort and stolen glances his way. Part of him wanted to ease the tension, to fall back into the simple rapport they'd once shared. But a larger part of him remained angry, hurt by their failed relationship and the awkwardness that now defined their interactions at work. Every day at the precinct was an exercise in avoidance, a careful dance of professional courtesy masking personal pain.

"Hey." Leila broke the silence. "Are you sure you're okay with this? I can talk to Sergeant Quinn and see if they can send me somewhere else."

TJ forced a slight smile to his face. "It's fine."

Didn't really matter if he was or wasn't okay. He had a job to do, and if that job was to play host to his ex-fiancée, then he'd do it without hesitation. "Besides, there's nowhere else close by to send you. The next safehouse is a county over and Quinn wants to keep you close to help with the case. Let's just get there, find this guy and get back to normal."

He leaned forward and snapped on the radio.

"You mean back to avoiding each other at all costs?"

Her response stung, even if it was true. Was that what they had become? Two people who once planned a future together, now reduced to awkward encounters and forced professionalism?

"Something like that."

His answer induced another long silence as they climbed into the mountainous hills. Manicured landscapes gave way to lush forest and thick vegetation—an isolation he craved when the world dumped too much on his plate. He breathed in deep, trying to calm his racing thoughts.

"You don't have to do this, you know," Leila changed lanes to go around another slow car. "Quinn could assign someone else to oversee my protection detail."

"I'm a cop, Leila." He rolled up his window. "If Quinn wants to keep you safe at my cabin, then I'm going to do my job." He ran a hand through his hair, feeling the beginnings of a headache forming at his temples. "I'm just tired. That's all. I really don't feel like talking. Can't you understand that?"

"Of course."

Leila turned up the radio, filling the car with a classic country song about a man washing away the memories of an ex-girlfriend. Despite the song's message being a testament to his current situation, TJ was grateful for the noise. All he needed was another thirty minutes. Then they'd be there and they could retreat to their private rooms without having to interact.

They crested the final hill and started their winding descent. More snow was swirling now and sticking to the road, demanding Leila's full attention. Her speed made him uneasy as his anxiety rose with each increased tick of the needle.

"You need to slow down." He sat up straighter. "These roads are icy and dangerous."

Before Leila could respond, a massive delivery truck roared past on the left, cutting them off as it swerved into their lane. TJ's heart pounded as Leila slammed on the brakes. Her foot went to the floor.

"That's not good." She gripped the steering wheel tighter and pumped the brakes again. Still nothing.

"I thought you said this truck was in good shape."

"It is. Mom had it inspected last month. I don't—" Leila's words cut off as the guardrail blurred past them, a stark reminder of the sheer drop waiting if they lost control.

"Watch out." TJ gripped the dash in front of him.

They gained on the delivery truck. Leila swerved into the passing lane at the last second, missing the rear by inches. The sudden movement sent a jolt of adrenaline through TJ's system, his body tensing as if preparing for impact.

Leila turned on her hazard lights and pressed

the horn. The cacophony pierced the air, a desperate plea for safety. Cars began pulling to the right shoulder as her speed climbed past eighty miles per hour.

TJ gripped the door handle, his knuckles white, fighting against the urge to grab the wheel himself. "Try the emergency brake."

Her foot pressed the smaller pedal to the floor with a sickening snap. The sound seemed to echo in the car, a death knell for their chances of a safe stop. "Nope. Nothing."

His stomach tightened as their last hope vanished. The speedometer rose past ninety, then a hundred. His mind raced through solutions, none of them ideal. The four-lane highway narrowed ahead, further complicating their dire situation. He scanned the road, looking for any opportunity, any way out of this death trap.

Leila dropped the transmission into the lowest gear, but their speed continued to climb. The engine whined in protest, the smell of burning oil adding to the acrid scent of fear in the car. They navigated another hairpin turn, the tires squealing in protest. He could feel the car's balance shifting, teetering on the edge of control.

"I won't make the next one." Leila motioned ahead.

The upcoming curve held a sharp right that hugged the mountain's contour. Beyond it lay nothing but open air and a drop that made his blood run cold.

"There," he said, pointing to a runaway truck ramp on the right shoulder. "Steer into the sand."

He saw Leila hesitate, her face pale. In that moment, TJ was struck by how vulnerable she looked, so different from the confident detective he worked with every day. "But the—"

"We have no other choice." He knew the impact would be brutal, but it was their only shot at survival.

Leila nodded, wrenching the wheel hard. They fishtailed as they hit the incline, and without airbags, he braced himself for impact.

The truck bucked to the left, shuddered and rolled three times through the rough surface of the ramp. Metal crunched with the ground. Glass shattered.

The abrupt deceleration slammed TJ forward, then around, his seat belt digging deep into his chest. His head snapped back, then forward, connecting hard with the dashboard. Pain exploded behind his eyes as darkness crept in at the edges of his vision. Leila's panicked voice called his name before unconsciousness claimed him.

Time became fluid, reality slipping in and out of focus. TJ drifted in a haze of disjointed thoughts and fragmented sensations.

He tried to move but his body refused to cooperate. He drifted in and out of consciousness, aware of Leila's presence beside him but unable to communicate. A part of him wanted to reassure her, to tell her he was okay, but the words wouldn't come.

As sirens approached in the distance, TJ's foggy mind latched on to a troubling thought. Their brakes had failed—was it just a terrible coincidence, or something more sinister? The case they were working on, the killer targeting Leila…could he have sabotaged their vehicle? The only time they'd left the truck unmonitored was at his house when she picked him up. He hadn't seen anyone around but his mind struggled to work through the fog of pain and confusion, searching for any clue that might explain their near-fatal accident.

The car door opened, and TJ felt a rush of cold mountain air. Voices, urgent and professional, floated around him. Men in uniforms assessed the situation. He felt hands on him, checking his vitals, probing for injuries. The pain in his head intensified as they moved him, and he bit back a groan.

"TJ? Can you hear me?" Leila's voice cut through the fog, closer now. Her hand slipped around his fingers, a sensation both familiar and strange. "Stay with me, okay? Help is here."

He wanted to respond, to squeeze her hand and let her know he was still fighting. But his body remained uncooperative, trapped in a limbo between consciousness and oblivion. As the paramedics worked to stabilize him and prepare him for transport, TJ clung to awareness with all his might.

Whatever the truth behind their accident, TJ knew one thing for certain—their journey to his cabin, and this investigation, had just become far more complicated. As he was extracted from the wreckage and loaded onto a stretcher, TJ made a silent vow. He would recover, find the truth, and keep Leila safe—no matter the cost to himself.

The ambulance doors closed, and TJ felt the vehicle begin to move. As the adrenaline of their ordeal faded into exhaustion, one question remained clear in his mind: who would protect Leila now?

FIVE

Leila's heart pounded in her chest, each beat a reminder of the chaos she'd just survived. The wreck was still a blur of dust and panic as she stayed behind to answer questions from the police. All she wanted was to get to the hospital and check on TJ, but duty kept her tethered to the scene.

She closed her eyes as she sat in the passenger seat of Quinn's SUV, trying to steady her breathing. The twisted wreckage of her father's classic truck winched forward onto a flatbed, the screech of metal on metal grating her already frayed nerves. The passenger side took the brunt of the impact and frightening visions of TJ's lifeless body plagued her mind. Firefighters used the jaws of life to cut him out, the image seared into her memory.

Quinn opened her door, his face etched with concern. "Okay. Paramedics are ready to check you out."

She raised the lever on the seat to sit up, wincing as every muscle in her body protested the movement. Fresh cuts stung her skin from the shattered windshield and the rancid taste of metal in her mouth testified to the violence of the crash.

Leila exited the vehicle, her legs shaky as her feet sank into the deep sand of the runaway truck ramp. She grabbed on to the back door to keep from losing her balance. With all her strength, she managed to make the necessary steps, each one a small victory against the pain and exhaustion threatening to overwhelm her.

Red and blue lights surrounded the ramp. A conglomerate of medical personnel and investigators moved around the scene, while a spattering of press and curious onlookers gawked from the sidelines. Cameras flashed as she inched toward the ambulance, but Leila paid them no mind. Her thoughts were consumed by TJ and his condition.

He was usually so full of life—a twinkle in his green eyes and a quick laugh when warranted. Leadership had awarded him with multiple medals as a cop, his bravery and dedication to the job unquestionable.

In truth, Leila often thought he would've made a better detective, but they had given her the job instead. With everything going on, she was starting to think her superiors had made a mistake. TJ would never be in this mess if he were working the case.

She struggled to think clearly, her mind racing with a million terrifying possibilities. What if he didn't make it? What if he didn't fully recover from his injuries? The thought of TJ, vibrant and strong, reduced to a shell of himself was almost too much to bear. Another person she cared about was hurt because of her, and the weight of that guilt pressed down, making it hard to breathe.

"Leila."

A man's voice shouted her name from the crowd. She glanced over but kept walking, assuming it was just another journalist trying to get his shot for the local news.

"Leila. Over here."

She looked again, this time spotting a man waving—large, muscular and tall, with the streetlights at his back. He walked through the deep sand toward her with little effort, his powerful frame seemingly unaffected by the treacherous terrain.

Quinn's hand moved to his weapon, his instincts kicking in as he shone a flashlight into the man's eyes. "Stop right there."

The man raised his arms into the air, his biceps bulging with the movement. "I just want to see if she's okay. I'm her trainer. A personal friend. Tell him, Leila."

Recognition dawned on her, cutting through the fog of confusion and pain. "Vince? Is that you?"

A smile stretched across his face, familiar and yet somehow unsettling in the harsh light of the emergency vehicles. "Yeah. I saw your wreck. I headed up the mountain and turned around to come back. I didn't realize it was you until you got out of the SUV."

Quinn lowered his light and walked a few steps away to give them some privacy, though Leila could tell he was still on high alert. Vince Cardello moved closer, his expression a mix of concern and curiosity. "Are you okay?"

"I am but my partner had to go to the hospital. I'm hoping to get there soon and make sure he's all right."

"Do you need a ride? I'm happy to take you."

Leila hesitated, torn between her desire to get to TJ and her professional obligations. "I'm not sure my sergeant would let me go right now, but can you give me a few minutes? We have a few more procedural things to discuss."

Vince looked toward Quinn, then back to

Leila. "Of course. I'll go get my truck and pull it closer. I wouldn't want you to have to walk too far."

"That would be great, thank you."

As Vince traversed the deep, sandy ramp with no apparent effort, Leila couldn't help but marvel at his strength. It was undeniable, but then again, she wouldn't expect any less from a man who worked out every day and trained others for a living.

After Leila gave her statement recounting the terrifying moments of the brake failure and received the all-clear from the paramedics, she found Quinn.

"I'm ready to go to the hospital."

"If you give me a few more minutes, I'll drive you," Quinn said, looking up from some paperwork he was signing.

"No need. Vince is going to take me."

Quinn's eyebrows raised slightly. "Your trainer?"

"Yeah. I've known him for years. He's vetted. No worries."

Her sergeant eyed Vince, who was waiting by his truck, then looked back to her. His expression was unreadable, but Leila could sense his reluctance. "Fine. I've got a few more things to tie up here and then I'll be there."

She walked to Vince's truck, each step a reminder of the ordeal she'd just been through. Hauling herself inside, she felt a wave of exhaustion wash over her. Vince waited for her to buckle up before he pulled onto the main road, the truck's powerful engine rumbling to life.

A dim glow from the dashboard lights filled the cab. Leila glanced over at Vince as he stared straight forward, maneuvering through traffic. A chill ran through her, though she couldn't place why.

Sure, he was her trainer, someone she'd known for years, but something about him triggered a sense of unease. Her attacker's face had been covered, but she remembered his strength, his muscular build. It wasn't Vince... was it? The thought seemed ridiculous, and yet she couldn't shake it.

"Do you travel the mountain often?" Leila readjusted her shoulder strap.

"Every day to work," Vince replied, his eyes on the winding road ahead. "I have a house in Old Fort and have to drive to Asheville to the gym."

The uneasy feeling relaxed a bit. Her sister had profiled their killer to live nearby or even in her neighborhood. Old Fort was a good distance away. "That's quite the trek. I'm surprised you don't open a gym closer to where you live."

Vince shrugged. "Nah. I'm happy where I work and I don't want the headache of running my own place. Then I'd be the one responsible."

"True." He seemed innocent enough, but Leila pressed on, her detective instincts kicking in despite her exhaustion. "What about your family? Do they live nearby?"

"My mom lives about ten minutes from the gym in Shadow Forest and I've got a brother that lives one county over."

The chill returned. "Shadow Forest is the same neighborhood where I live."

"Not surprising. Most of my clients live there."

"Are y'all close? With your family, I mean?"

"I guess so. As close as any other family." He shot her a narrowed glance, his tone sharpening a bit. "Why all the questions? Are you writing a book or something?"

Leila backpedaled, realizing she might have pushed too hard. "No reason. Just trying to keep my mind off the wreck and TJ. I'm really worried about him."

"I'm sure he'll be fine."

She glanced out the passenger window to

the other side of the mountain where she and TJ had nearly lost their lives. The guardrail seemed to mock her, a thin metal barrier between safety and oblivion. "I'll try to make it into the gym soon. Work has been really busy lately."

"Yeah. I saw all the news coverage about your promotion," Vince said, his tone softening. "Congratulations on being the first female detective for the Shadow Creek Police Department."

"Thanks. I'm quite honored to have the position."

He smiled again, and this time it seemed genuine. And yet, there was something hidden behind his eyes she couldn't quite place.

The tragic circumstances of the wreck and the trauma of her attack were getting the best of her. She had to get a grip. The fact Vince had been traveling up the mountain at the same time as her wreck didn't make him a murderer. Not every man in her life was a serial killer. Then why did this man she'd known for years suddenly feel like a stranger?

He steered the truck around another bend, then exited the highway. Town lights came into view and Leila felt a mix of relief and apprehension. Soon, she'd know TJ's condition.

Soon, she'd be back in the thick of the investigation. And soon, she'd have to face the reality that someone out there wanted her dead.

"We're almost there," Vince said, breaking into her thoughts and dispersing the silence.

"Thanks for doing this. I really appreciate it."

"Of course. That's what friends are for, right?"

Friends. The word echoed in Leila's mind. Was that what they were? She barely even knew the man despite their years of working out together.

The truck came to a stop in front of the main hospital entrance, and Leila reached for the door handle. She paused, turning to Vince one last time. "Thanks again."

"Anytime. This world can be a dangerous place, ya know, and it's good to know when people have your back."

He reached into the back seat and pulled out a bottled water. The fabric of his tank top fell forward revealing a small scar on his chest. The raised area was in the same location as her victim's pin wound but his was healed over. "Here. Best to stay hydrated."

She took his gift then stepped onto the sidewalk, holding the door open. "One last question."

"Shoot."

"Were you ever in the military?"

"Yes, ma'am. Specialist with the 82nd Airborne. Didn't you know that?"

"Afraid I didn't." She forced a smile, gave him a small wave then closed the door as he drove away. With easy access to all her victims, the blood pin scar on his chest and his presence at the wreck, Vince Cardello just earned a spot on her suspect list.

TJ's head throbbed and the sterile, white walls of the hospital room seemed to close in on him. Three pills of migraine medication had done little to alleviate the pain in his head despite their administration almost thirty minutes ago.

At least his spine had been cleared of any injuries. If only he could do the same with the swirling memories in his mind. Not that he could remember everything. Only bits and pieces of the crash, the high mountain speeds and tons of dust.

Leila sat next to him, her eyes filled with fear and concern. "Good. You're awake."

He tried to sit up but the bolt of pain stopped him. "My head—"

"You have a concussion. Just try to rest."

The sliding glass door to what looked like

an emergency room bay slid open and a tall man dressed in wrinkled green scrubs and clog shoes walked into the room. "We got the results back from your CT scan. There is no brain hemorrhage, so we can release you back home. You'll need to take it easy for a couple of weeks. No driving or operating heavy machinery, and you need to stay out of work for at least a week."

"Not work? I can't do that."

The man took a step closer to TJ's stretcher and placed a hand on the railing, his expression tightening. "You don't have a choice. If you decide to go against my orders, it will take you twice as long to recover and your work will suffer. I'm guessing that could be dangerous for you and your colleagues considering your line of work."

The doctor was right, but he had to guard Leila. He'd figure something out even if he had to rely on her sisters a bit more to help, at least for the next few days.

TJ didn't want to argue, so he nodded his head in agreement. He figured he better save his strength for the tense conversation he'd have to have with Leila and Sergeant Quinn. Convincing them to let him remain on duty would be a fight.

The doctor seemed satisfied. "The nurse will

be in soon with your discharge papers and pre-scriptions for nausea and migraine meds. Fol-low the directions exactly as written. Let your brain rest for at least a week before you resume normal activity."

Another quick nod. The sooner he got out of here, the sooner he could get back to work.

After the doctor exited the room, TJ pushed himself up to a sitting position and ignored the wave of nausea that swept through his body.

Leila placed her hands on his shoulders. "What are you doing? Did you not hear the doctor?"

"Yeah. He said I was being discharged." He motioned to a green bag sitting on a chair. "Can you hand me that? I need my shirt and shoes." He was thankful the nursing staff had left his pants in place. TJ removed the pulse ox monitor from his finger, slipped off his gown and ripped the heart monitor patches from his chest, taking a few hairs with the adhesive.

Leila frowned, handed him his T-shirt, and headed for the door.

"Where are you going?"

"I'm going to give you some privacy."

Not like she hadn't seen him in his swim trunks before, but that was when they were to-gether. "Not without a guard you're not."

TJ replaced the hospital gown with his T-shirt and stood from the bed. A surge of dizziness swayed his position. He closed his eyes and reached for the railing. Leila's warm touch was on his arms in an instant.

"See? You don't need to be moving so quickly. Sit back down."

He leaned against the bed for a moment until his vision evened out, and then raised his gaze to hers. They'd not been this close since their breakup. "I'm fine."

Her muted vanilla perfume wafted between them and he fought the urge to kiss her. They'd been clear when they broke up. Once they called it quits they were done with anything other than a platonic, work relationship.

He turned away. "Really, I'm good."

She stepped back to give him some room to slip on his shoes. "Why do men have to be so stubborn? Can't you do what the doctor says, just this once?"

Her cheeks turned pink when she was frustrated. He missed that cuteness about her. "Now, what fun would that be?"

She lightly smacked at his arm. "Thomas James Snowe. Am I going to have to get mean and force you to follow the doctor's orders?"

He kept tying his shoe. "How about this?

I'll promise to follow doctor's orders if you promise to listen to me so I can keep you safe." Maybe he could milk his concussion a bit to get her to cooperate with him.

"Deal."

He stood. "The cabin awaits."

"You need to go home and rest."

"My cabin is the most relaxing place there is."

"Are you sure?"

He wasn't, but when Sergeant Quinn told him to take her there, he really didn't have another choice. At least it was safe. She was a sitting duck in the middle of an ER department. "Doc told me to rest and Quinn wants you there under guard. Seems like we both need my old mountain hideaway."

"I just figured—" She shook her head. "Never mind. To the cabin, then."

The glass door scraped open again and Sergeant Quinn stepped into the room. Leila moved away from TJ's side. The older man shot them a curious look but didn't comment on their posture.

His gaze shifted to TJ. "You okay?"

"About to be discharged."

"But he has to take it easy for a few days."

"Understood. Think you can drive him back

to the precinct. I had patrol bring you another car." He tossed Leila the keys. "We need to talk."

"Sure, but what's so urgent?"

"We found the man who tampered with your brakes. He's in holding. I want the two of you to question him."

"I've got someone I want to look into more as well."

"We'll head there now." TJ gathered the rest of his things, signed his discharge papers and exited with Leila. The pain from his migraine was nothing compared to the rage he planned to release on their suspect. If he was the one threatening Leila's life, he'd make sure to do everything he could to put him behind bars for a very long time.

Leila stood by the precinct's coffee machine watching the dark liquid drain into her favorite mug, wondering when the antiquated contraption had last been cleaned. Footsteps shuffled behind her and stopped. She turned. TJ leaned against the doorframe, reminding her of past times when they'd shared conversations in the break room. Even with a white bandage covering the gash on his head, the man still sent flutters through her.

"That stuff will kill ya."

She smiled. "At least I'll be awake when it does."

He moved to the fridge in the corner and pulled open the door. "Still take vanilla creamer?"

"I do." She lifted her mug from the counter and returned the carafe to the burner. "I'm surprised you remember."

"Your coffee order is etched into my brain forever."

He'd almost been her forever, but this job had taken that future from her.

TJ snapped the lid closed. "Quinn's ready for us."

"So that's why you're being so nice. To hurry me along?"

"You always were a slowpoke, especially when you get a cup of coffee."

"I do some of my best thinking watching the slow flow of our outdated machine."

"Well, we've got a tough nut to crack in the interrogation room and the clock on how long we can hold him is running out."

She took a sip and savored the flavor. "How are *you* feeling?"

TJ moved to the door. "Like I hit my head on a metal dashboard after your truck slammed into a thousand pounds of sand."

"Funny."

They continued down the hallway until they were at Sergeant Quinn's door. TJ knocked and their superior waved them inside. "Good, you're here."

"What do we need to know before heading in with this guy?" Leila took another sip from her mug and settled into one of the chairs across from her superior's desk.

"We reviewed the security footage from TJ's house last night and the man you're about to interview is on the video."

TJ leaned forward. "He got a name?"

"Kieran Murphy. Either of you know him?"

"Never heard of him," Leila said, sitting up a bit straighter.

Quinn scrolled through his computer screens. "Appears to be a lowlife with a rap sheet a mile long—assault charges, felony drug possession and theft. Anything that will give him a quick buck to keep his drug addiction satisfied."

"And that's why he cut the truck's brake line?" TJ asked.

"As far as we can tell. We need to know who paid him, how he gets his orders and if he can or will ID the man calling the shots." Sergeant Quinn nodded his head toward the room across the open area the detectives called the bullpen and handed her his file. "Room 1. He's all yours."

Leila flipped through the still photos and documents. She handed one of the images to TJ. "He was there all right. Looks like he cut the lines when we went inside to get your bag."

They headed straight for the interrogation room. This man had tried to kill her and she wanted to know why. She let her hand rest a moment on the cool metal knob, inhaled a calming breath, then pushed the door open. TJ followed her inside and leaned against the back wall, giving her space to take the lead.

Harsh white light cast gray shadows along the man's face, making him look older than his thirty-three years according to his file. He seemed familiar. A lingering scent of sweat, mixed with a mild skunky smell, emanated from his clothing as he sat handcuffed to the table. There was no mistaking his identity. She had met Kieran before, and her mind swirled with images from the attack.

She took a quick seat, feigning confidence even though panic and rage filled her. The sparse furnishings in the room did little to provide a reprieve from the immediate stress.

Kieran barely looked up, his attention focused on his thumbnail as he picked at his cuticle. Leila stared at him without a word, fighting the trembles in her legs. With an inhale, she flipped open the folder, shuffled through the pages and images, then stopped on one of Kieran bent down beside her father's old truck. She slid the photo in front of him.

"Is this you?"

Kieran barely glanced at the picture. "Can't tell. The image is blurry."

"How about this one?" Leila slid a clearer image of the man's face in front of him.

He shrugged.

She pulled out her phone and retrieved the security camera picture of Kieran from the morning he attacked her. She placed it in front of him. "I've got evidence of felony assault on a police officer, conspiracy to commit murder and kidnapping. When I get DNA results back from the two dead women we've found, we'll have enough to press two counts of murder one charges against you. You're looking at well above fifty years in a maximum-security prison. Still want to remain silent?"

His dark eyes met hers and narrowed. From behind yellow teeth, his foul breath almost made her gag.

"I didn't kill anybody."

"Funny you picked that crime first out of all the others. Would you like to confess to the previous crimes I listed?"

"I'm not a murderer."

"So you don't get your kicks from strangling women? What then? You just deliver them into the hands of some other killer?"

He returned to picking at his thumb.

"You really expect me to believe that when I have two dead female bodies in my morgue with your DNA all over them."

"I take them and drop them off. I don't know what happens after that."

"What do you mean you *drop them off*?" TJ pulled out the chair beside her with a scrape and took a seat.

"He pays me. I take the package and drop it where he tells me to."

"What's his name?" Leila asked.

The man shrugged.

"You don't know his name? The name of the man who pays you to abduct women for his kicks."

"He never told me."

Leila fought the urge to hit the man and instead pulled the financial records Quinn had given her. "He paid you—" she glanced at the sheet one more time for effect "—over 300K in total deposits. All of them dropping into your account the same day each of my victims were abducted. Not to mention the ten thousand you received on the same date my brake line was cut. Seems to me this friend of yours is setting you up to take the fall. Making sure all the evidence points at you if the cops get too close. We arrest you and he goes on living his free life and carrying out his murders. You really want to protect someone like that?"

He leaned back in his chair and crossed his arms. "I told you. I don't know his name."

TJ lifted the financial sheet and dangled it in front of the man. "Then how does the system work? He pays you to do a task, correct?"

Kieran nodded. TJ continued, "Then how does he contact you with instructions?"

"I get a message on my phone with the task and the amount. I reply with my answer. Once the job is done, the money shows up."

TJ stared at him for a moment, then exited the room, leaving Leila alone with her handcuffed attacker. She figured Quinn was right on the other side of the one-way window if she needed help.

Leila stood, paced to a wall to keep some distance from the man, then leaned against it, hands in her pockets. "Why does he want me dead?"

His dark eyes met hers and a sly smile brushed up the corners of his mouth. "I don't know. It's not like we have a cup of coffee and gab about the meaning of life."

Leila moved to the table and placed her palms down on the surface, leaning toward him, despite fear coursing through every fiber of her body. She wasn't about to let him know she was scared out of her mind. "I'm going to find him and when I do, you'll go down with him. North Carolina is a death penalty state. Might want to think about that for a while, Mr. Murphy."

"Maybe so, but I haven't killed anyone and last I checked North Carolina doesn't enforce capital punishment for kidnapping. I'll be out in a few years and made enough to take care of my kid's college fund." His yellow teeth took center stage. "And your guy. He's connected. You'll never catch him."

She straightened, surprised Kieran was a father and had a kid in college. "So he's wealthy enough to pay you and have a top-notch legal team at his disposal. Thanks for the tip."

She turned to exit the room but he continued.

"He won't stop coming for you. Besides,

you're already too late. He has his replacement. You're just the cherry on top now."

A cold chill swept down her spine. If his words proved true, and she didn't find the killer soon, another woman was going to pay the ultimate price. Problem was, Leila had no idea how to find her in time.

SIX

The unmarked SUV rumbled up the isolated mountain roads as TJ stared straight ahead. Snow came down in a steady pace. A few more hours of this kind of weather and the roads into the cabin would be unpassable without their four-wheel drive and they'd be snowed in, together. Great.

Not a word had been said since they left the precinct, and TJ glanced over at Leila back in the driver's seat. She stared straight ahead. Something was clearly on her mind, and she'd yet to share the details with him.

Whatever their suspect had said to her at the end of the interrogation had spooked her. Even he could see that, especially when she didn't put up a fight to Sergeant Quinn's orders for her to go to a safe house. It was so unlike Leila to acquiesce without argument, but TJ hadn't been there. He reviewed every statement, every answer that he did hear and regretted leaving the interrogation room to retrieve the man's cell phone. By the time he'd returned, Leila and Sergeant Quinn were already planning her leave. The sudden change in her cooperation left him with an uneasy feeling in the pit of his stomach.

He made a mental note to log in and look at the interrogation footage when he got a chance. He wanted—no, needed—to know what Kieran Murphy had said to scare her into compliance. The Leila he knew was fearless, stubborn to a fault. Seeing her this shaken unsettled him.

The thick forest pressed in on both sides of the narrow road. Wind whipped the trees into a frenzy and the snow intensified as they climbed into higher elevations. The weather seemed to mirror the turmoil TJ felt inside, an icy storm brewing both outside and within. "Are you okay?"

She glanced at him, then back to the road, her eyes never lingering on his face for more than a second. "Yeah. Why?"

"You're unusually quiet. What did he say to you?"

Leila slowed for an upcoming curve. "There's another victim."

He sat up straighter and triggered another

spike of pain through his head from his recent concussion. "Kieran told you that?"

"Pretty much. And I don't know how to find her. Or this psychopath either."

"You think he's talking about Kitty St. Claire or someone new?"

"I don't know but he's ten steps ahead of us, and I don't know what to do."

The defeat in her voice was palpable. He wanted to reach out and comfort her, but the gulf between them seemed too wide to bridge. Instead, he focused on the case. "We'll work on it when we get to the cabin. Our first priority is to keep you safe."

"And how are we going to do that?" The skepticism in her voice was clear.

"We've got a whole host of weapons there and cameras around the entire property. Very few people know about my cabin. You're the only one—"

He stopped, not wanting her to know how much he used to love her. Still loved her, if he were honest with himself. Their relationship was over, and he had to put past feelings aside if he wanted to do his job. But in moments like these, with Leila so close and opening up to him, he struggled to remember why they had fallen apart.

"And what about the woman or women he has now?" Leila asked, her voice cutting through his thoughts. "How do we find them?"

She steered the car around a sharp bend in the road, the tires slipping a little on the snow. Gray clouds hovered over the forest, dampening their visibility.

"I don't know yet. But you can't help them if you're dead."

"Maybe we need backup. With you injured, we need to make sure you rest while we're here too."

"With this storm moving in, I doubt anyone can reach us. We can handle this."

"We did use to be quite the team," she said. "Professionally, I mean."

Her words gave him a glimmer of hope. "I don't know. I thought we were pretty good personally too."

A hint of a smile played across her lips. "Ya think?"

For a moment, the tension between them eased. But the reprieve was short-lived. As they rounded the next bend, Leila hit the brakes hard, the SUV skidding slightly on the slick road.

"Did you see that?"

Leila's body leaned across the console as

she peered out the passenger-side window, the light scent of her lavender perfume wafting in his direction. TJ shifted, following her line of sight, hyperaware of her sudden proximity. "What is it?"

"I thought I saw a man."

He looked back at her, the nearness of her body fighting for his attention. "I didn't see anything."

She looked up at him for the first time since stopping and must have realized her invasion of his personal space. Leila straightened, putting distance between them once again. "My mind must be playing tricks on me. Never mind."

She repositioned behind the wheel and inched forward, her movements cautious. "This case is getting the best of me."

TJ glanced back to the area she had been searching, his cop instincts on high alert. Movement caught his eye, and he relaxed slightly. "It's just a deer. Look."

Leila followed his gaze, and another smile lit up her expression. "A baby. With its momma. Looks like they're hunkering down to ride out the storm."

Something moved in his side mirror and TJ's blood ran cold—the shadowed outline of a truck inched through the trees. Leila's body tensed next to him, and he knew she had seen it too.

Without a word, she hit the gas, and the SUV lurched forward, the glow from her headlights cutting through the darkness as they rounded the curve ahead.

"There's a truck behind us."

TJ's mind raced. Had they been followed? Only Sergeant Quinn knew they were here. "Yeah. I saw. They must be tracking us somehow. No way they knew about my cabin before we came here."

"This drive seems longer than I remember," Leila said, picking up speed.

"We've got another three miles to go." TJ tried to keep his voice calm despite the growing unease in his gut.

A pair of headlights blazed to life behind them, the intense glare flooding the interior of the SUV. Leila pressed the accelerator to the floor, her tires spinning on the current incline. The vehicle behind them was large, but TJ couldn't make out any details other than the fact that the beast of a truck was closing the distance between them.

Without warning, the driver rammed into the back of their car. TJ's seat belt tightened against his chest, and Leila fought to keep the tires on the road.

The truck came at them again, slamming into their left corner. TJ's head whipped forward with the impact, his vision blurring momentarily. The back tires of the SUV fishtailed and Leila lost control, sending them careening into the woods. Trees whizzed past as they veered down an embankment. She dodged hitting anything head-on, and TJ prayed their increasing momentum wouldn't roll the vehicle.

"Watch out." TJ gripped the dash in front of him, bracing for impact.

Another drop in the terrain sent them airborne for a heart-stopping moment before they slammed back to earth. The SUV continued down the embankment, trees pounding the metal sides of the car.

After what felt like an eternity, they came to a jarring halt. Heavy silence filled the cab, broken only by the sound of the rushing river in front of them mixed with his ragged breathing. Pain pounded in TJ's head, his earlier concussion undoubtedly exacerbated by the crash. But at least he was conscious and able to move this time. He reached for her hand. "Leila. Are you okay?"

In the darkness, he could barely make out

her form. With shaking hands he unbuckled his seat belt and fumbled for his phone. His fingers stumbled upon the charger cord, and he lifted the device into his lap. With one hit to the side button, the screen lit up the inside of the SUV with a whitewash glow. Leila stirred next to him.

"Are you okay?" he asked again, his voice hoarse. "Anything hurt?"

"I can't move my ankle." Pain resonated through her voice. "It's lodged underneath some of the crushed metal. It hurts."

"Don't worry. I've got some cutters in the back in my bag. Let me get them."

TJ pushed against his door, the metal groaning in protest. As he stepped out, cold water rushed around his knees, and a new fear gripped him. He turned back toward the cab and let the light from his phone fill the interior of the SUV. Water was slowly seeping in on the driver's side, the level rising with alarming speed.

He raised his gaze to Leila, her eyes wide with renewed fear as she realized their predicament. "Get me out of here before I drown."

The SUV had landed at the edge of the Green River, and if he didn't move quickly, Leila would be trapped in a sinking car.

"Hold on," he called to her, fighting against the current to make his way to the back of the vehicle. "I'm going to get you out. Just stay calm."

But even as he said the words, TJ knew the situation was far from simple. With the icy river filling the vehicle, they both were in danger of hypothermia. The current tugged at his legs, threatening to sweep him off his feet. And somewhere in the darkness, their pursuer might still be out there, waiting to finish what he'd started.

As TJ struggled to open the rear hatch, his mind raced. Even if he got her out, with an injured ankle the climb back up the embankment would be a challenge. If their attacker was still in the woods, they'd have trouble escaping him. They'd have to float downriver and approach his cabin from a different angle. They'd be wet and cold.

With a grunt of effort, he managed to wrench the hatch open. Water immediately poured in, and TJ knew their time was running out. He grabbed his bag, fumbling with the zipper as he searched for the cutters.

"TJ, the water's rising."

"I'm coming." He grasped the tool he needed

and sloshed back to the driver's side, fighting against the current with every step.

"Hold still. I'm going to cut you free." Adrenaline coursed through his veins. "But as soon as I do, we need to move fast. The current's strong, and I don't know how much longer the SUV will stay in place."

Leila nodded, her jaw set with determination. "Do it."

TJ began to work, the cutters slicing through the twisted metal that trapped Leila's ankle. The water continued to rise, now reaching her waist. The SUV groaned and shifted slightly, the current threatening to pull it further into the river's depths.

"Almost there." He made the final cut and wrapped an arm around her waist. "Let's go."

She winced as he pulled her from the vehicle and into the water. The cold hit a physical blow, stealing their breath. The current immediately caught them, sweeping them downstream.

"TJ, we need to get to shore."

"He'll be waiting for us at the top. We need to move further down so we can get to the cabin without being seen."

"But the water is freezing."

"We won't be in it for long." He scanned the

shoreline as they floated for the safest route back up the cabin. "Can you swim?"

"I think so."

"I've got you." TJ took her hand in his. "Just don't let go and kick with your good leg if you can."

TJ fought against the river with all his strength, keeping Leila's head above water as he aimed for the shore. The snow continued to pour down, making it hard to see more than a few feet ahead. A large branch hung low over the water. TJ reached out, and his fingers brushed the rough bark as he fought to get a solid grip.

"Climb up." He boosted her onto the branch, then pulled himself up. They rested on the branch for a moment, shivering against the temperatures. Snow continued to swirl around them as the river raged below. They weren't safe yet. They still needed to get to shore, and their attacker could still be out there.

"We need to move," TJ said, helping Leila to her feet. "Can you make it to shore?"

Leila nodded, her face a mask of pain and determination. "I'll manage. Let's go."

They made their way along the branch and to the pebbled riverbank. The crunch of tires on gravel sounded above them.

TJ held up a hand. "Wait." As they scrambled for cover in the underbrush, their ordeal was far from over. The night was dark, they were wet and freezing, and somewhere out there, a killer continued to hunt them.

Leila's body shook, the cold seeping into her bones. Her hands and feet had long since lost all feeling, and each step was an agony of effort. Exhaustion pulled at her, threatening to keep her seated on the pebbled beach. TJ's hand gripped hers, pulling her upward with a determination she couldn't match.

He stopped when she didn't budge. "The truck's gone but may come back. We need to keep moving." His voice was steady despite the tremor she felt in his hand.

"I can't," Leila said, her words slurring from the cold. "I'm so tired."

TJ knelt beside her. His eyes, usually so guarded around her now, were filled with concern. He wrapped an arm around her waist and hoisted her to her feet. Leila leaned against him, her legs refusing to support her weight.

"You have to move. That will help keep you warm."

She shook her head. Strands of her wet hair

had turned icy. "My clothes are frozen, and I'm so cold. I just need to rest a little longer."

TJ's arms wrapped around her, pulling her close. The gesture was so familiar, so comforting, that for a moment Leila forgot about the cold, about the danger. She forgot about the years of hurt and misunderstanding that had driven them apart.

He leaned in, his breath warm against her ear. "I know you're cold, but if we don't keep moving, then hypothermia will take over. You have to push through the exhaustion."

She felt the burn of tears in her eyes as TJ's gaze dropped to her lips, and Leila wondered if they were as blue as his. He couldn't be much warmer with the wind cutting through his wet clothes and the temperature dropping by the minute.

"You're not a quitter, Leila." His voice was low and intense. "And I'm not going to lose you again."

His hands cupped her face and he placed his lips on hers. Soft and urgent, as if to convince her of more to come in the future. The familiar sensation, the warmth it sparked within her, was impossible to resist. Leila gave in to the moment, rushing back into the comfort of TJ's embrace.

As they broke apart, her mind whirled. Maybe the near-death experience had scrambled her brain, but in that moment, she didn't care about the past, about the hurt they'd caused each other. She'd missed this—having someone to love her, support her, to be her person. If only they could find their way back to each other.

He slipped his arm around her waist, and Leila leaned into him as they started moving again. The cold wind knifed through her soaked clothes, but TJ's body provided a barrier, a source of warmth she needed.

They inched their way up the steep, slippery embankment. Leila's breath came in ragged gasps, especially as feeling began to return to her injured ankle. Every step sent jolts of pain from her foot to her chest.

"Just a little further."

Leila squeezed her eyes shut, gritting her teeth against the pain and cold. "How much farther?"

"Not much. Keep thinking warm thoughts, okay?"

The snow intensified and the wind howled around them, but Leila was determined to make it to the cabin. She focused on putting one foot in front of the other, leaning heavily on TJ for support.

"Remember our first date?" TJ asked.

"We went ice-skating on the pond behind my parents' house."

"And your sisters crashed our party."

"I wish they were here now. With warm blankets and hot coffee."

As they crested the last hill before reaching the road, TJ continued. "You were so sure the pond was frozen solid, and then the ice cracked. You dropped through."

"And yet I think I'm colder now than I was then," Leila said, her teeth chattering.

He pulled her closer. The exertion of supporting her up the hill had heated him up, and she wanted nothing more than to curl into his warm body and never let go.

"I didn't know how to skate and had no idea how to get to you without falling through too," TJ said. "Your sisters came running, made a human chain and pulled you from the pond. I'd never seen your lips so blue. Until tonight."

"Is that why you kissed me?" Leila surprised herself with the question. She was sure hypothermia had addled her brain, because no one in their right mind would question the kiss they'd just shared, but thinking about his lips on hers earlier was the only thing keeping her going.

TJ stopped for a moment, his breathing labored. He ran a hand through his wet hair, a gesture so familiar it made Leila's heart ache. "I didn't want you to give up."

"On us or life in general?" Her heart raced despite the cold.

TJ shook his head and repositioned her arm across his shoulders. "We need to keep moving."

"You didn't answer my question."

"Let's not do this right now."

"Haven't we waited long enough?"

TJ's expression hardened, the walls she knew so well coming back up. "There's a serial killer targeting you, and I'm cold, wet and tired. Are you ready to move or not? We don't have much further."

The tenderness of the moment by the river was gone, replaced by the professional detachment TJ had perfected over the years.

"Well, it worked." Bitterness filled her tone.

"What?"

"You got me moving. That was the goal, right? Just doing your job?"

"What's that supposed to mean?"

"I'm your assignment. The task you must protect. Even if that requires a reluctant kiss to keep me moving."

"That's not what—"

"I guess I should be grateful instead of surprised. After all, you *are* one of Shadow Creek's finest."

TJ didn't respond although his jaw tightened at the sarcastic tone of her words. Maybe the cold made her too harsh but she was tired of hoping there might be something left to salvage. They always found a way to hurt each other, even if he was the last person she wanted to offend.

By the time they reached the three-bedroom log home, the horizon was starting to lighten, a dim glow breaking through the gray snow clouds. Leila followed TJ inside, watching as he cleared each room, making sure they were safe.

He grabbed wood and kindling from the covered porch, then nodded toward one of the bedrooms. "I think there are still some dry clothes in there. Don't take a shower yet, though. The hot water will be too much of a shock to your system. We need to warm you with blankets and a fire first."

Leila made her way to the bedroom she had always used when they were engaged. Opening the closet door, she was surprised to find her things still hanging inside, untouched. The sight brought a lump to her throat. Had TJ been unable to remove her things, or unwilling?

She grabbed her old cream cashmere sweater and a pair of ripped jeans. Every movement sent pain through her body, especially her ankle, now swollen to three times its normal size. Leila was sure it was sprained. She needed medical attention, but right now, all she wanted was warmth and sleep.

After brushing and drying her hair, Leila made her way back to the great room. Flames danced in the rock fireplace, and TJ had pulled the old, lumpy couch right up to the hearth. He handed her a steaming mug of coffee and took a seat in a chair next to her.

"You can have the couch."

Leila stretched out as much as she could, propping up to drink the hot beverage. The liquid warmed her from the inside out, and she felt exhaustion settling over her like a heavy blanket. With each sip, she studied TJ's profile, his green eyes sparkling in the firelight. He kept his gaze straight ahead, not meeting her eyes.

Setting the mug on the hearth, Leila felt her eyelids growing heavy. For the first time in days, she felt safe enough to relax. TJ's presence, despite the tension between them, was comforting in a way she hadn't expected.

As she drifted off to sleep, Leila caught TJ looking at her. She was too tired to question him and closed her eyes instead. His lips on hers played over in her mind, stirring up long buried emotions. If she lost him again, the damage to her heart would be far worse torture than any serial killer could invoke.

Leila's eyes fluttered open, and she was momentarily disoriented. The fire, down to only embers, cast a soft glow across the room. She was still on the couch, with a warm blanket draped over her. *TJ.*

She turned her head, expecting to find him on the other end of the couch, but he wasn't there. Panic gripped her for a moment before she spotted him by the window, his silhouette outlined against the light of dawn.

He must've sensed her gaze because he turned, their eyes meeting across the room. For a moment, the years fell away, and Leila saw the man she had fallen in love with—strong, protective and fiercely loyal. But then reality crashed back in, bringing with it all the hurt and misunderstanding that had driven them apart.

"How are you feeling?" he asked.

"Better." The bone-deep cold had receded,

replaced by a dull ache in her muscles and a throbbing pain in her ankle. "How long was I asleep?"

"A few hours." He moved back to the couch and sat on the edge. "The snow has stopped, but we're not out of danger yet."

Leila nodded, pushing herself into a sitting position. "What's our next move?"

TJ ran a hand through his hair, a gesture Leila recognized as a sign of frustration. "We need to figure out who's after you and why. And we need to do it before they find us here."

They weren't just two people working through their complicated past. A calculating killer hunted them and always seemed to be one step ahead.

"I should call my sisters," Leila said, reaching for her phone before remembering it was probably at the bottom of the river.

"Already taken care of." He motioned to an old rotary phone on the wall. "I used the landline to call Quinn. He's bringing a team up here and is letting your sisters know you're safe. He should be here in a few hours."

She nodded and held his gaze for a moment before he looked away. "You should eat something, regain your strength. I'll see what I can find in the kitchen."

As he stood to leave, Leila caught his hand. "TJ—" She paused. "About our kiss…"

His expression softened for a moment before the professional mask slipped back into place. "A motivation tactic. That's all. We should focus on keeping you safe."

She didn't believe him but what choice was there if he wanted to dismiss their connection. With a release of his hand, Leila leaned back on the couch and closed her eyes. He was right—they had a killer to catch, and their personal feelings had to take a back seat. She just hoped that her heart would get the message. Being near him in this cabin was more painful than her injured ankle.

SEVEN

Leila's eyes snapped open. She remained motionless on the couch, trying again to place her surroundings. Her gaze swept across the room, taking in the old couch, rock fireplace, and TJ asleep in the recliner.

How long had she been out this time? Darkness filled the large windows again, so she must've wasted most of the day in slumber. Memories of the night's terrible crash rushed to the forefront of her mind with startling clarity—her injured ankle, the icy river waters and TJ's kiss. The weight of his lips still pressed into her mind.

Leila stood, blanket in hand, triggering a surge of pain in her ankle. She needed ibuprofen and recalled seeing a bottle in the vanity. Using the couch as a crutch, she limped toward where TJ slept. He stirred, gave a soft snore and settled deeper into the worn chair. His face, relaxed in sleep, bore no trace of the worry and tension that had marked his expression earlier. She draped the blanket over him, then hobbled toward the hallway.

A muffled thump from the back of the house stopped her cold. Leila held her breath and prayed she was imagining things. The cabin's wooden walls seemed to amplify every sound, making it difficult to pinpoint the source. Then another thump sounded, louder this time on the other side of the mudroom door. They were not alone. She needed her weapon, but the police-issued 9mm was at the bottom of the Green River.

She returned to TJ, shook his shoulder, and placed a finger to his lips when he startled. "Someone's here."

While TJ retrieved his weapon from his holster, Leila grabbed one of the fireplace pokers, the cold metal reassuring in her grip. She followed TJ toward the garage door.

Her injured ankle protested with each step and she leaned on the poker as her cane, gritting her teeth in order to keep moving. She had to back up TJ. No telling who or what was on the outside.

They approached and listened. Everything was quiet except for the panicked notions swimming in Leila's head. Maybe she'd imagined the noise. Her mind had been working overtime, conjuring up threats from every shadow. Now she'd awakened TJ. She'd never live down the embarrassment if their inevitable intruder ended up being a stray cat.

Several minutes passed without any noise or action. TJ shrugged his shoulders. "Must've been an animal." He headed back toward the recliner and placed his gun into the holster before taking a seat.

Leila turned toward the couch when the door burst open with a resounding crack. She pivoted and swung her weapon at the masked man lunging toward her. He was fast. An iron grip seized her neck and squeezed. The poker clattered to the floor, the sound echoing in the sudden silence. Her body landed against the wall, triggering white stars in her vision.

Leila blinked to refocus, her heart pounding in her ears. In the light of the flames, a raised fist swung toward her face. With quick reflexes, she blocked the blow, feeling the impact reverberate from the punch.

A blur of motion slammed into Leila and her attacker from the side. A tangled heap of bodies and thrashing limbs sprawled across the floor. TJ grappled with the assailant as Leila rolled out of the way, gasping for air.

The two men traded blows across the hardwood floors, scattering furniture in their wake. Fists flew and harsh grunts of exertion filled the room, as firelight cast their shadows into twisted murals on the walls. The sound of flesh hitting flesh echoed, punctuated by the crash of overturned furniture. TJ managed to restrain the man in a headlock and squeezed, his arm clamping tighter with every second. "You picked the wrong person to mess with."

"TJ—stop." Leila's voice was hoarse from the assault on her throat. She grabbed his handcuffs from the table. "We need him alive."

Unconsciousness overtook the man, and TJ lowered the intruder to the floor. "And I need you alive," he said, his eyes meeting Leila's with an intensity she'd only witnessed when he took down resistant offenders. "Hurry. I want to have him restrained before he wakes up."

Leila tossed him the cuffs as he fastened the man's arms around one of the four-foot-thick posts holding up the ceiling and duct-taped his ankles together. She stared at the man's face, searching for any familiar features. TJ sat back against the wall, his chest heaving from the exertion. "Do you know him?"

She shook her head, still reeling from the attack, and took a seat beside him on the floor.

Her ankle throbbed along with her head. "Not at all," she said. "You think he's another hired hand like Kieran?"

"Most likely."

Leila remained on the floor as TJ searched the intruder's clothes and extracted a cell phone from the man's jacket pocket. With a quick glance in her direction, TJ used the unconscious man's finger to unlock the device. He scrolled through the messages, then stopped. Tension tightened his jaw. Whatever he found wasn't good.

"What is it?" she asked, leaning forward. "Is there a high bounty on my head?"

TJ's hesitation only increased her anxiety. His Adam's apple bobbed with a hard swallow as he read.

Package secured. Sedated in the van. Rendezvous at drop-off point ETA 2 hours. Target acquired.

Leila pushed up from the floor. "I'm the target?"

TJ shook his head and turned the screen toward her. "Dani."

What little strength she'd regained from her rest, drained from her body at his revelation. She stared at the photo of her twin sister on the screen. "That can't be. She's too smart. Too quick."

"The text is time-stamped yesterday."

Leila snatched the phone from his hand, her fingers shaking as she read the message again. The realization hit her like a physical blow. "That's what Kieran meant when he said he'd found a replacement and I was just the cherry on top. He took Dani since he doesn't have me."

Leila moved to the intruder and kicked him in the side. "Wake up and tell me where she is!" She shoved the phone in front of his face. "What did you do with my sister?"

The man didn't respond but kept his expression stone-cold. Leila straightened and moved to the fireplace, retrieving TJ's weapon, then strode back across the floor, pressing the barrel to the man's head. "I asked you a question."

"Leila." TJ's voice echoed through the vaulted room. "Give me the weapon."

"Not until he tells me where Dani's at."

The man leaned his head back against the post and closed his eyes. "Got nothing to say."

Heated rage spread through Leila's body into her trigger finger. She pressed the barrel further into his skin. All she had to do was pull and even the score a little bit. So many female bodies. Sisters, mothers, wives, friends all gone for a paycheck. Surely, the man behind all this deserved to lose one of his soldiers. A hand squeezed her arm.

"Don't do this, Leila," TJ said. "Give me my gun."

This monster in front of her deserved death, but if she pulled the trigger, TJ would be disciplined regarding the use of his gun, and she'd go to prison for murder. She relented and moved back to the couch. Leila pulled out her own phone and dialed Dani's number. It rang and rang, each unanswered call increasing her distress. He had her. The man who had killed two women so far had not only Kitty St. Claire but also her sister, and it was all her fault. Dani's voice mail played but Leila didn't leave a message.

TJ had moved across the room by the fireplace and held his phone to his ear. He must be talking to Sergeant Quinn. He ended the call and faced her.

"They know about Dani. Just found out a few minutes ago. Quinn has every unit available searching the parkway for her."

Leila lowered her body to the couch, numb, not sure how to respond.

"Dani's strong." TJ continued. "She'll fight,

just like you. And we won't stop until we find her and Kitty St. Claire."

Leila wiped tears from her cheeks. "I know we'll find them. I just want to find her alive."

The fire crackled and their suspect moaned.

She looked over at him, rage filling every fiber. She stood and lifted the poker, placing the end into the fire for a few seconds. She'd make him talk whether he wanted to or not.

"What are you doing?" TJ asked.

Without answering, Leila moved to the suspect and held the poker close to his cheek. She wanted him to feel the heat on his skin, scare him into talking. The man's eyes widened. "Tell me who has my sister."

TJ crossed the room in two strides, placing his hand over hers. "You can't do this. You'll lose your job."

"Watch me." She moved closer, the man leaning his head as far from her torture tool as possible. "He knows where my sister is."

She stabbed at his face but TJ offset her movement, the end of the poker hitting the beam above the man's head.

"I won't let you—"

A loud knock rapped the outside door. Leila met TJ's determined gaze, then lifted her hand from the poker, stepping back from the suspect and moving to the foyer.

Cold wind swirled inside as Quinn entered. "I'm so sorry about Dani."

Leila closed the door behind him, still numb from the news. "You have a way to find her?"

"We have all units searching. They've been searching since we found out." Quinn nodded toward their captive, handcuffed on the floor behind them. "How'd he find you?"

"Must've followed us or tracked our cell phones," TJ said as he returned the poker to the fireplace then moved to the open kitchen and started another pot of coffee. "He tried to run us off the road and then broke into the cabin."

"I'll check your vehicle for a tracking device. If he found you, then others can too."

"The vehicle's in the river at the bottom of the bank."

"Well that's not good. I need to make some calls." Quinn disappeared into the back bedroom while TJ brought Leila a cup of hot tea.

"Are you going to tell Quinn what I did?" Leila asked.

"Hadn't planned on it. But don't ever do that again. If we want to find Dani then we can't have you getting fired."

Quinn returned and slid his phone into his

pocket. Leila sat up and placed her mug on the coffee table. "Any news?"

"According to Detective Clark," Quinn said as he sat in the chair across from her, "Dani's assistant called earlier today and said she went to check on a lead yesterday morning but never came back. They filed a missing person report at eleven-thirty tonight. So our units have been searching for three hours."

"And Kieran didn't give a name?" TJ asked.

"Still sitting silently in our jail cell."

Heavy footsteps thudded on the cabin's front porch and TJ pulled his weapon from his holster. Quinn held up a hand. "It's okay. Just some of my investigators." TJ exchanged a look with Leila as Quinn let the men inside.

"You definitely had a tracker on your car," the taller detective said. "We were able to tow it out of the river and will take it back to the precinct tracker and all. Must have been waterproof 'cause the crazy thing was still working. Anyway, we'll have one of the officers put it on their car and drive it around to different locations. That way our killer will think you've left the cabin. He will expect us to move you after the attack anyway and this will keep him chasing us instead of you."

"Sounds like a plan," TJ said. "Then he won't send any more of his hired assassins to come here."

"Exactly."

"That doesn't help my sister." Leila paced to the window. "He's got her. That's what Kieran meant about finding a replacement. She's my twin sister. What better substitute could he find than her?"

TJ threw another log on the fire. The temperatures had dropped during the last few hours and the cabin was cold again. He glanced at his watch. 5 a.m. The sun was just starting to peak above the ridge line and the search for Leila's sister would start soon. "Anything we can do to help find her?"

Quinn moved closer to the fireplace. "Yeah. Stay here. I need to put all my resources on finding Dani. If you are out there and something happens to you, I have to pull officers away from finding your sister. I don't think you want that. Am I right, Leila?"

She nodded. "This is my fault. I should've been more up-front with her. Told her all the details of my case. I didn't want to alarm her and now she's gone."

TJ lifted the poker and stirred the coals to help the log catch fire. "It's not your fault.

He's a psychopath who preys on women." He straightened and put the poker back in the holder with a clang. "You can't go blaming yourself for the evil choices of a serial killer. Dani is a smart investigator, and you know as well as I do, she'll follow any lead to the remotest parts of the earth to put a criminal behind bars. She's not one to let anyone get away with murder if she can do something about it."

"We all have that Kane sister stubbornness, which is why we often find ourselves in danger." Leila paced back to the couch, her fingers clenched into fists. "Dani knew better than to chase a killer without backup. Why didn't she tell someone? All of us are in law enforcement. We could've helped her."

TJ stepped in front of Leila, forcing her to stop and look at him. "That Kane sister stubbornness is how I know Dani's still alive."

Leila met his gaze, a flicker of hope breaking through the despair. "You think?"

"Yeah. Just like I know we will find her. Dani's too tough, too smart to let this monster win. She's out there, and she's fighting. We just need to find her."

Quinn cleared his throat, drawing their attention back to him. "TJ's right, Leila. If anyone can outsmart this killer, it's your sister and you. But we need to move fast."

A call crackled over Quinn's radio, breaking the moment. "We've got a situation at the precinct that needs your attention."

Quinn turned down the volume on his radio and dispatched two of his detectives to fetch their assailant. "I've got to go. I'll take the intruder with me and process him back at the precinct."

Leila followed the two men toward the door. "Did anyone see Dani get taken? Maybe a witness could ID our killer."

"You know as well as I do, even if they did, he would just be another hired gun like this guy." The sergeant motioned to the intruder the detectives were escorting out the door. "The man behind these killings is cautious and smart. Until we can trace these finances and get an idea where the money's coming from, he's just a nameless face out there."

"He'll make a mistake eventually. And we'll be ready," TJ said.

"We need to dig deeper. I'm coming with you." Leila walked back toward her bedroom. "Give me just a minute to get my things. If you could drop me at Dani's office that would be great. I want to go through her case files.

We're missing something and I've got to find the connection. I can't do that locked up here in this prison."

"Leila—" TJ reached for her arm.

She shrugged him off. "I'm going to pack my things. I'm not going to sit around while Dani's in danger."

Quinn held up a hand. "Did you not just hear what I said? You're his number one target. I'll have to send more officers to keep you safe which takes away from Dani's search. Is that what you want? Besides, I can have Dani's case files emailed to you."

TJ motioned to Leila. "*Why* is she his number one target? He'd have to know her, right? Maybe we've been looking at this all wrong."

"How so?"

"We've been looking at all the other victims, trying to find a connection. We've never looked into Leila's history, the past paths you've crossed and why he's selected you to be 'the cherry on top.' Why you? He has to know you."

"Or my father. That's the only connection Dani or I have to the military."

Quinn ran a hand over his face. "Your dad's been dead for a while, right? What would be the point in targeting you and your sister?" Her superior shook his head. "I think TJ's right. You must've had a run-in with this killer before. Maybe years ago, before he escalated to murder?"

"Then that would make me the reason he started killing. Seems like I'd be able to figure out who he is or remember him from that time in my life."

"Not necessarily." Quinn shot her a look as if they shared a private secret. "Trauma does strange things to memory."

The slow emphasis Quinn placed on his last statement along with the look he shot Leila, paused the conversation. The silent exchange happening between them excluded TJ from some hidden detail or past story they shared.

"Am I missing something?" TJ asked.

"No," Leila said, a little too quickly for his comfort.

TJ turned his gaze to Quinn. "You want to tell me what's going on? What do I not know?"

"I think it's time to tell him, Leila. Not only to help you but to help your sister. This could be our guy."

"What guy?" TJ was still in the dark and he didn't like secrets, especially when they were part of a case he was working.

Leila's eyes turned glassy. "There was one

man from my past. I've never told anyone about him or what he did to me except for Quinn." Her gaze met TJ's. "Not even you."

A tear slipped down her cheek and she swiped it away.

A rush of heat flushed through TJ but he fought to remain calm. "What happened?"

Leila lifted the wet paper towel from the counter and pressed it to her eyes. Every muscle in TJ's body wound tighter with each passing second of silence.

"After Dad passed, I struggled with his death and turned to alcohol to help ease the grief. I made the mistake of frequenting a bar one night and met a man there who was charming. After returning from the restroom, I found my drink was much stronger. I didn't think much about it then, but now I know he drugged me. He took me outside, assaulted me and tried to strangle me. A car pulled into the alley and he left me lying there. The couple who found me called 911."

"When did this happen?" TJ asked.

"Right after Dad died."

"We were dating then."

Leila nodded.

"And you're just telling me about this now?"

She didn't respond and he continued. "Was the guy in the military?"

She shrugged her shoulders. "I think so. He had a tattoo but I don't know for sure."

So many of their relationship troubles made sense in a flash. After her father's death, he'd tried to support her—after all, he'd been through a parental death years before—but she'd always put up a wall. A new distance developed between them. She blamed it on grief from her father's death but she never seemed to get better. Now he knew why.

"And you think the man who attacked you on your jog is the same as this guy?"

"Could be. I don't remember who he is, though. Not his face or his name."

No wonder Leila blamed herself. If the killer was the same guy, she'd experienced everything he'd done to their victims except for death and now he had her sister. TJ prayed they found Dani in time. If this monster took her sister's life, then Leila would never recover.

She turned and disappeared into the bedroom. TJ fought the urge to follow and comfort her like he used to do. But things were different now. *They* were different. He'd blamed himself for their breakup, thinking he'd messed everything up over her promotion and his relationship issues due to his past. He never realized Leila had secret pains she was keeping from him, hindering their future.

"She needs you," Quinn said after her bedroom door closed. "I know things have been complicated between you two since your breakup, but right now, she needs you more than ever."

"How did I miss this? How could she tell you and not me?"

"She's still hurting."

"I know. I just don't know how to handle all of this."

Quinn nodded "You love her, don't you?"

"Some part of me will always love her."

"That's enough for right now. You're what she needs."

"What about the next steps to find Dani?" TJ asked, changing the subject. If they didn't find her before the killer took her life, then he'd be a constant reminder of this dark time. No relationship could ever survive that.

Quinn sighed. "We've got forensics combing the scene, but this guy is meticulous. No fingerprints, no DNA."

"We know his motive now," TJ added. "That's new. He's someone from her past and has to be somewhat wealthy to pay hired hit men to abduct women. And we know Leila is the one that got away. He's killing these women either to get back at her or taunt her."

"We're not going to let that happen." Quinn pulled his car keys from his pocket. "He's getting bolder, more confident. Try to see if she can remember anything else. The more we know, the sooner we find her sister and stop this maniac."

"I doubt she'll open up to me. She needs her sisters."

"They're at the farm with their mother. Apparently, Lila Kane is taking the news about Dani pretty hard."

"Understandable."

Quinn nodded. "But Leila's here with you. She'll talk if it means finding her sister, and you should be the one to have that conversation with her."

His superior's phone vibrated and he read the screen, his face pale.

"What now?" TJ asked.

"They've found Dani's car abandoned on the Blue Ridge Parkway and there's a body nearby."

TJ glanced at Leila's bedroom door. "Is it Dani?"

"They don't know." He clicked the screen

black. "Looks like we will need her at the crime scene after all."

Quinn handed TJ his keys then pulled them back when he reached for them. "Do not wreck this one."

TJ smiled. "I'll do my best not to."

"I'll catch a ride with one of the detectives. No rush. Get there when you can and try not to be followed."

"Will do." TJ opened the door for his boss. Cold, moist air filled the room.

Quinn inhaled. "They're calling for a big one."

"Isn't that what all the weathermen say and then we get very little."

"I think this one's different. Already dumped several inches here and the second wave is going to hit mid-day." Quinn glanced at his watch. "That gives us about six hours to get the crime scene investigated before nature covers everything in a blanket of snow."

The man zipped up his coat. "See ya both in a few?"

TJ nodded, closed the door and watched through the window as the man left. Tall evergreen trees whipped with the increased wind and he pulled up his weather app on his phone. Quinn was right. A large snowstorm *was* moving in by mid-afternoon. He just hoped the killer didn't find them before the blizzard hit.

TJ walked to Leila's door. Her muffled sobs discouraged him from interrupting but he had to give her the news about Dani.

He wanted to comfort her, tell her everything would be okay. But after hearing Leila's confession, he wasn't sure he could promise that anymore.

Strong, cold winds lashed against the cabin walls and creaked an eerie sound. Somewhere out there, Dani was fighting for her life. And somewhere out there, a killer was watching, waiting, playing his twisted game.

TJ clenched a fist and rapped against her door.

"Come in," she said and he let his hand rest on the knob, hesitating. They *would* find Dani. They *would* catch this psychopath. And maybe, just maybe, in the process, he and Leila could find their way back to each other. But first, they had to survive the nightmare that was only just beginning.

EIGHT

TJ studied Leila's face as they stood at the edge of the Blue Ridge Parkway, taking in the grim crime scene below. A small opening through snow-covered evergreen trees provided the only view. A winding river fell across mountain cliffs, casting a mist around the bottom of the snow-covered location. Under any other circumstance, this would be a winter wonderland but not with a woman's dead body lying at the bottom.

Investigators preserved as much of the scene as possible. Whether the body next to the falls was Dani or another victim, they both deserved justice and an uncorrupted crime scene.

Yellow crime scene tape outlined a trapezoidal area where several investigators worked in an effort to beat the snowstorm headed their way.

"You ready?" TJ nudged her elbow with his.

"Not really."

Her gaze darted from one investigator to another, watching their every move.

"It's not Dani." He took her hand in his, hoping his touch might provide some comforting reassurance.

"You don't know that."

"Yeah I do."

He led her down the path of footprints left by other investigators. To his surprise, she didn't pull away.

"What if you're wrong?" Her fingers squeezed his as she almost slipped but regained her balance.

He could be, but this wasn't the time to let his doubts show. He had to remain positive for her. "We can't rule anything out until we get down there and take a closer look."

Her jaw set in that determined way TJ knew so well. She was compartmentalizing, pushing her emotions down in order to focus on the task at hand. It was an essential skill for a detective, but one TJ worried she leveraged too often, especially during their past relationship.

Without another word, he continued to pick his way down the steep slope, boots crunching in the snow and gloved hands grabbing low-hanging branches for support in icy spots. Leila didn't hesitate but moved with him.

As they neared the body, the scent of decay wafted strong. They signed the log sheet and moved under the crime scene tape. TJ held his breath even though he'd been exposed to the smell of death a hundred times before. The scent never got easier to bear.

One of the investigators nearby gave them a somber nod. "Young female, mid-thirties." He gestured toward a white sheet covering the body. "Bruises around the neck. Most probable cause is strangulation, but we're waiting on the medical examiner to confirm."

TJ pulled back the sheet covering the body. His eyes raked over every detail—bruising, lividity, scratches, as well as the blood pin embedded into the woman's chest. Broken branches around the area indicated she'd put up a fight and lost.

"It's not her." Leila knelt in the snow. "It's not Dani."

Dr. Singer, the medical examiner, appeared from a makeshift tent they'd set up. Her auburn hair was wrapped in a tight bun at the nape of her neck, and her aqua-colored glasses gave her a unique look while she typed on her phone. "It's Kitty St. Claire."

"The jogger whose husband reported her missing?" Leila stood and swiped the snow from her pants. "My sister was working on her case."

"The same one, according to her fingerprints. I was hoping you could tell me more about her." Dr. Singer looked up from the screen.

"From what Dani told me, she was happily married, had a group of good friends, and liked to jog every morning."

"And the pin?" Dr. Singer asked.

"It's a blood pin," TJ pointed at the pin with his gloved hand. "The other victims have them too. We think this is part of the killer's MO."

"Right into their chest like this one?"

"Afraid so." TJ nodded. "Some military groups conduct blood pinnings as a way to bond their units together although leadership frowns upon the practice."

Dr. Singer lifted the victim's arm. "Marks on her wrists. She was bound."

TJ viewed the deep abrasions. "She fought back hard."

"She certainly tried. Those are defensive wounds." Leila motioned to the bruises on her forearms.

"Unfortunately, when we find female assault victims, those markings are common," Dr. Singer said.

TJ noted the area around the body. Snow covered the ground but had been disturbed by multiple footsteps made by investigators. "Who was the first to find her? Did they note if there were any footprints before your team arrived?"

"One of the officers found her after an anonymous tip was called in. I'll have our forensic photographer send you the first photos."

TJ stepped back, taking in the entire area. A reflection, off to the side in the trees, caught his attention, and he bent down. "A button," he said, holding up the small metallic object shaped like a heart. "Could be from the killer's clothing."

Leila reached out and took the object from him, turning it over in her hands. "I've seen this before." She stepped back to where he found it and brushed some of the snow away with her foot, then picked up another item. "A piece of a pink flannel shirt."

"The victim's not wearing a pink shirt." TJ grabbed a couple of evidence bags.

"Because the shirt's not hers." She took the bag from his hand and slipped the fabric inside. "It's Dani's."

"Are you sure?"

"Positive. Which explains why her car is in the area too."

"Do you think she witnessed the attack? Followed him here or, worse, he brought her here?"

Leila nodded, her fingers trembling as she closed the plastic bag. "Unfortunately. Dani loved this shirt. It was her favorite, and she wore it all the time."

Dr. Singer's team moved in to place the victim in a body bag. "At least your sister's not the one dumped here. We still have time to find her before he does this to her."

"Have you classified him as a serial killer yet?" Quinn asked as he walked up. TJ hoped Dr. Singer would say no, but the look the woman shot his superior confirmed what he knew.

"Not yet, but that's what we're dealing with. He marks all his victims with the pin, and I've got three victims now that we've found Ms. St. Claire." Dr. Singer scrolled on her phone. "A Stacy Greene, Lori McCoy and now Kitty."

Leila stood frozen, staring at the dead body. "And he has my sister."

TJ could only imagine what was going through her head. He turned to Quinn. "We need to call in the state bureau of investigation. If the killer brought Dani with him or caught her surveying him, then they could still be in the area. We need to lock this place down and comb every inch for any more evidence that could point to Dani's location."

"One step ahead of ya," Quinn said. "I've already made the call and given the team their grid search areas. We've secured another mile radius. Every potential piece of evidence will be cataloged—fibers, footprints, disturbed foliage and more."

Flashlight beams bounced into the dark recesses of the forest as officers spread out to carry out their sergeant's orders. TJ just hoped it wasn't too little too late.

A sense of dread settled over him. The thought of Dani in the hands of this killer made his stomach churn. He glanced at Leila, who was now talking to one of the search team leaders, her face a mask of determination. He admired her strength, but he also knew the toll this was taking on her.

As hours passed, the search yielded little new information. The forest seemed to have swallowed up any traces of Dani or the killer into the gray snow clouds deepening above them.

Sergeant Quinn approached TJ and Leila. "This crime scene appears different than the first ones. There's more blood. The victim was beaten and strangled where the others didn't have a bruise on them other than their necks."

Leila held up the baggie with the piece of her sister's shirt inside. "I think I know why. Dani was here. I think she tried to save Kitty but was too late."

Sergeant Quinn reviewed the evidence they'd found and shot a look at TJ. "And now he has her."

"Looks that way." Leila's voice was steady despite the fear TJ could see in her eyes.

"So you think Dani tracked the killer here, followed him into the woods hoping to save Kitty St. Claire. When she saw him with Kitty, they fought with him, and then he took your sister with him after he killed Ms. St. Claire."

TJ nodded. "From the extended search, it looks like he chased Dani back to her car, where investigators found it abandoned on the road. I think that's where he caught up with her."

"I'm headed there next. It's not far from here, right?" Leila asked.

"At the top of the hill, next overlook up." Sergeant Quinn paced back and forth, then stopped. "Why didn't he just kill her here too?"

Leila lifted her gaze to his. "Because he's going to use her to get to me."

The words sent a cold shiver down TJ's spine. The thought had never occurred to him that Dani was leverage to get to Leila, but with her past assault and the fact she didn't die, it helped the killer's motive take shape. They had to figure out who this man was, but with Leila unable to remember details, he could be anyone.

Faded moonlight streaked through the trees, reflecting off the unmistakable shape of the green Honda sedan parked off-road right next to the mountainous overlook and trailhead to the falls. If Leila had visited during a clear day, expansive views of layered mountains would stretch out before her, but at night, everything past the bright crime scene lights bathed Dani's car in a sick yellow hue. Her sister was out there somewhere. Most likely in the hands of a serial killer. Her mind tortured her with memories of past victims from former cases. The atrocities that serial killers inflicted on their prey filled her with nausea. She prayed Dani would never experience such torture. *God, please protect her.*

She trudged up the last of the trail toward her sister's car. TJ walked behind her without a word. They were both still processing the murder scene, trying to connect the dots to give them any advantage to find her sister. There had to be a connection. Something she was missing. The undeniable brutality of the murder made her stomach turn and she prayed that if the killer did take Dani's life before they found her, she wouldn't experience such a horrendous death. But knowing her sister, she'd fight until there was no fight left in her, no matter the cost. Not a way any woman, or man for that matter, should ever die.

Dani's car looked remarkably intact from the outside. No visible dents, smashed windows or other signs of a violent struggle. She walked around to the driver's-side door and aimed her flashlight beam inside. Her initial flutter of hope was extinguished when she peered through the window. There, on the seat, she saw small but sickening red dots. She stepped back and inspected the open door. More blood on the handle.

"Investigators believe she walked down this trail when she arrived and followed the trail into the woods, looking for Kitty." TJ motioned toward a narrow path off to her left. "They think he chased her back to the car and caught up with her here."

"That explains the blood."

"It could belong to the killer. They're running it through the database now."

As tiny as the droplets appeared, their implications were enormous—proof that her twin sister had been taken and no telling what else. She couldn't even finish the thought and squeezed her eyes shut, struggling against the wave of dizziness that washed over her. The warmth of TJ's hand landed on her shoulder.

"You don't have to do this, ya know? We can go back to the cabin. The snow's coming down harder now and—"

"She's my sister. I want to work the case. You would do it if it was your brother."

"Doubtful. My brother and I don't really talk anymore. Not since Dad was killed."

"How come? Seems like a tragedy like that would've brought you together." Leila couldn't imagine not talking to her sisters even for one day. However, TJ's life had been rough growing up with his parents' divorce and then his dad's murder. No wonder he'd decided to become a cop.

"Long story. Not one I really want to get into."

She didn't push him, like he didn't push her. Not once had he asked about her past assault. She'd figured he would've had a barrage of questions as soon as Quinn left the cabin, but instead, he'd given her some time before he informed her about Dani. Maybe he didn't care especially since she couldn't remember the most important detail—the killer's identification. Was her assailant from back then, the killer now? She wasn't sure, but that was the only personal connection she had for the one that got away.

All she was able to wrap her mind around was Dani's abduction. She refocused on the details. "Stacy and Lori were both strangled. Both had the pin. Both were left near water off the Blue Ridge Parkway."

"And neither of them served in the military," TJ added.

"Maybe he did since he knows about the pins."

"Definitely his calling card."

Leila walked up the road, needing a moment.

TJ followed, touched her arm and stopped her ascent. "We've got to talk about the conversation at the cabin if we're going to find this guy."

The last thing she wanted to do was discuss the intimate details of her assault after her father's death. The whole ordeal had blown up her future with TJ. She hadn't been able to think, eat or focus on anything for months and now her past had caught up to her again. She should've told TJ what happened back then since they'd been dating, but it was easier to break off their relationship when she had the chance. "I know. It's not easy."

"If my questions get too hard, just say so and I'll stop, okay?"

She nodded and TJ continued. "What was the name of the bar where you were attacked?"

"Smoky Mountain Tavern."

"On State Street?"

"Yeah." She'd pushed him away so many times after her father passed and kept telling him she needed space. He had tried to be there for her, support her, but the guilt she carried was too strong.

"And you said you went alone that night?"

"I went alone most nights."

He sat up a little straighter. "Most nights?"

She'd never told him about frequenting bars and drowning her grief after her father passed away. She was able to show up for work, do her job and keep everyone at arm's length. "For several weeks after Dad passed, I stayed with my mom. She didn't take his death well. None of us did. She went to bed early and I went out. The bar wasn't far from the farm."

TJ's face flushed.

They'd been dating at least eight months, he'd proposed and she'd said yes. Then her father died. She poured all of their future plans right to the bottom of a low-ball glass. History.

He turned away from her, paced a few steps then circled back. "Why didn't you ever tell me? We were engaged and not supposed to keep secrets from each other."

Tears slipped down her cheeks again. "I was ashamed. I shouldn't have been there in the first place but I struggled to cope with my dad's death."

"That's when you're supposed to lean on the ones who love you and not push them away."

She dug the heel of her boot into the dirt. "Easier said than done."

The weight of his gaze was heavy on her and she didn't look up.

"Any other secrets I need to know about that might give background to this case? Any ex-boyfriends that might want to do you harm?"

"You mean other than you?" She shot him a quick glance, hoping the tease would lighten the tension of the moment but his expression lacked amusement.

The last thing Leila wanted to do was discuss her former love life with her ex-fiancé. She'd pushed all these details way down because she didn't want to think about them again, much less share them with TJ. "This is so weird telling you all this. We didn't even talk about past relationships when we were together."

"Maybe that was part of our problem. We both put walls up. But now your sister needs us."

He had a point and if going through her past helped her find Dani then she'd try her best. She'd never opened up much to anyone, even him. Maybe they'd had more problems than she realized. "I only had two semiserious relationships before you. Both were amicable splits."

"What about Dani? She have any vengeful boyfriends?"

"Only one but he was killed in a car crash a few years ago. She's not dated anyone since."

"Why not?"

"She's engrossed in her business. Her whole life is about helping women escape abusive relationships. That's why she left the precinct. As a private investigator, she believed she could do more than working as an officer. I suppose an angry husband or boyfriend of a former client could be seeking revenge on her."

Dani dealt with some scary men and often

told Leila and her sisters if she thought she was in danger. Several close calls came to mind but the threats on her sister's life only drove her all the more. Could the killer be someone who'd finally caught up to her?

Leila's phone buzzed and she pulled the device from her pocket. "Quinn emailed all of Dani's case files over. Maybe we should head back to the cabin and go through her most recent cases."

"We definitely need to start with Kitty St. Claire since that case is specifically tied to this killer and your sister."

They walked back to Quinn's loaner car, made the thirty-minute, silent drive back to the cabin and settled in on the couch. TJ had kept to himself and she wondered if he'd ever be able to look at her again without pity in his eyes.

Leila started her laptop and opened the file. She clicked through several screens—documents, financial records, alibis for Kitty's husband and others who had seen Kitty that day, testimonies from all of the woman's friends.

"This woman was clean as a whistle." Leila marked a couple of spots on the document. "She loved her husband, took care of her friends and ran a successful skin care business. Her only mistake was going for a jog by herself at four in the morning."

"Keep looking. There's got to be something there and even if there's not, we are going to find your sister. No matter what it takes...we'll bring Dani home."

"Alive?"

He didn't answer.

She clicked on a jpeg file and the photo opened, filling her screen. Leila leaned in closer. "Hey, look at this."

TJ scooted closer to her, sending a whiff of his muted spice cologne in her direction. "What is it?"

"Looks like a group photo of a hike to Graveyard Fields' upper falls." She pointed to the screen. "There's Kitty and her husband."

"Yeah but look who's behind them in the photo."

A cold chill spread through Leila's body. "Is that Pete? The security guard in my neighborhood."

"Maybe. The photo is so far away and his hair was longer then instead of the buzz cut he has now."

Leila pulled out her phone and scrolled through her photos from about a month before she was assaulted at the bar. She typed the word hiking into the search bar. Several group photos popped up and she paused, then extended the photo to zoom. Pete stood behind Dani and her, same long hair, same serious expression on his face. She turned the screen for TJ to view. "The day before Dad had his stroke, we went hiking with a large group from church. Pete was there. He asked me to meet him for dinner and I turned him down."

"Maybe Kitty did the same."

"Do you really think someone would kill due to getting turned down for a date?"

"We've had people kill over twenty dollars before. And he's not just killing the women he's abducting, he's assaulting them too."

She knew the statistics for abduction victims weren't good. Most only made their way home in a body bag. But until that became a reality, Leila had to keep moving forward. She inhaled and fought off another surge of tears. They needed to formulate some kind of plan, figure out where he had her sister. Somewhere out there, Dani needed her. Leila would never stop, no matter how long the hunt took or how dark the road ahead turned. Even if it meant giving up her own life to save her sister, she'd make sure to find Pete and make him pay.

NINE

Leila marked another red X on the well-worn map spread across the cabin's kitchen table. Three bright X's now marred the crumpled surface, each marking the location where the bodies were found.

Outside, the wind whipped, blowing snow. The heaviest part of the storm had arrived and the conditions were deteriorating by the minute.

TJ had built a roaring fire, made chili in the Crock-Pot and brewed a steaming carafe of coffee. She was much warmer than when they'd first arrived, and precious memories of the times they'd spent here as a couple distracted her from her main focus. If she wanted to find Dani in time, then she had to stop thinking about him.

Leila looked at her watch. Thirty minutes after eleven and TJ was wrapping up another call with Quinn.

"They're sending several units down toward Rosman but they are going to have to call off the search soon. The weather is getting too dangerous for them to be out."

Leila pressed the lid back on the marker. "Why so far south? That's at least an hour from where we found the last body."

"The officer who put our tracker on his car as a diversion spotted the same large black truck that ran us down the embankment. Same license plate number and everything. Quinn will call when there is more news but he wants us to keep working the case."

Leila popped off the marker top again and retraced the red X near Wildcat Falls, the first victim's location. She stretched and reviewed the map again. They'd been combing through Dani's case files all night trying to tie everything together.

"Look at this." She traced a disturbing pattern emerging on the map with her finger.

TJ leaned back in his chair. "All of their bodies were found near a waterfall off the Blue Ridge Parkway. We already knew that."

"But it's like he's encircling Graveyard Fields. See how all the bodies are around that central point. Even Kitty St. Clair was placed here, at Sunburst Falls…"

TJ pressed the tip of a marker and circled Graveyard Fields on their map. "Well, the name does warrant the crime, I suppose. Perfect for a serial killer and super creepy."

"We need to check the area."

"Quinn's units are south of that. They'd have to backtrack to Graveyard Fields, and they won't do that until this storm clears out."

She hadn't thought about the parkway closing but when the weather turned bad, the gates got locked. If they didn't hurry, then she might not be able to search Graveyard Fields' upper falls area. "Surely someone has a favor they can ask of the park service to let us through. If not, then you can drive me to the gate and I'll hike in."

"That's a long way."

"Not if I go up through the Davidson River area. We used to backpack all the time through those woods."

He shook his head. "Not during a huge snowstorm that's getting ready to dump at least a foot, maybe two, overnight. Quinn will never permit you to do something so rash."

"Rash or not, my sister's life is in danger and she'd do the same for me. You can either go with me or I'll go alone."

Leila walked into her former bedroom and started pulling her gear together.

TJ followed. "You don't even know Dani's there. We have an educated guess at best based on a few old photos. He could have her somewhere else. You're grasping at straws in desperation and it's going to get you killed."

"If he dumps her body before the storm, the snow will cover her for days. It will take us longer to find her. I can't do nothing. We're running out of time."

"This is exactly why Quinn should've taken you off the case completely. You're not thinking straight."

Leila tossed more warm clothes into her bag and grabbed the bedroll she kept on the top shelf. She couldn't believe TJ had kept all her things. "Maybe I am desperate." She glanced out the window. "Quinn's going to call off the search. The snow is getting heavier, but I have to try to find her."

"Graveyard Fields is an hour and half's hike on a good day. In a freezing blizzard it will take us twice as long. At least wait until morning. We can hike in then. He won't take her out in this weather—"

"He'll take her to the upper falls tonight."

"How do you know?"

"'Cause that's where Dani and I used to hike when we were in college. Plus, he's dumped every other victim at one of the falls. This is the best one in the area and the only one left circling Graveyard Fields."

"Let me call Quinn. Maybe he can get his units down there before they close the gates."

"We can't wait for them if they are at Sunburst Falls. It will take too long. We have to go find her now."

A tense silence stretched between them, the implication clear. TJ broke it first, scrubbing a hand down his face in agitation.

"We have to tell Quinn. That's protocol."

"You can tell him but I'm not waiting." Leila grabbed a large coat from the closet and found some of her old hiking boots. "By the time they get redirected, we can be there. It might already be too late for Dani." There was no way she was sitting here in this cabin after recognizing the killer's pattern. "I can't wait any longer, TJ. Not when that monster has my sister."

TJ stared at her for a long moment, indecision etched in the hard lines of his face. Finally, he gave a slow, grim nod of understanding. "Okay. Then we go out there together. We'll drive to the gate. I've got a park ranger buddy I can call who owes me a favor. He'll let us through but you have to stay with me the entire time. No running off and playing hero for your sister."

She made a swift move and wrapped him in an unexpected hug. "Thank you for having my back on this."

At first he stood frozen, then squeezed her closer, burying his face in her hair. "I've always got your back and I always will."

She leaned back to meet his gaze, wanting to kiss the man who always helped her when she needed him. But this was not the time. This was the time to find her sister.

TJ grabbed his keys, weapon and pulled on a warm coat and boots. He hoped Quinn's four-wheel drive would make the entire trip, but even then they were looking at a three-mile hike all the way to the upper falls. Maybe all for nothing. They really had nothing concrete that Dani would be there but he had to try for Leila.

Once in the vehicle, he called Sergeant Quinn on speaker. "We think we know where he's taking Dani tonight. The upper falls at Graveyard Fields. Y'all are too far south."

"You're breaking up. I can't—"

They lost their connection.

"Try the radio." Leila handed the device to him.

He wasn't able to connect with Quinn but

he talked with dispatch, gave them their location and requested backup.

"Might take them several hours, but at least we know someone will be following up with us."

TJ flipped on his wipers for better visualization but not much was helping as the storm grew more intense. "I don't know, Leila. This doesn't look good. If we slide off one of these mountain roads, we may be the bodies they end up finding."

"It's not ice. Just go slow."

"Why are you so certain this is where he's taking her and how do we know this is the exact day?"

Her fingers tapped her legs. "He likes to use a distraction like he did with the burgundy van he got you to chase and then circled back for me and Holly at the house. Then the black truck. I think it's another distraction, plus this is the only waterfall left around Graveyard Field that he hasn't hit yet."

"Except for the lower falls."

"Yeah but we will pass that on the way. We can check there too."

"I'm still not sure about the timing of this. Why tonight in the middle of the snowstorm?

Seems kind of insane to me, not that serial killers are known for their sanity, but still."

She hesitated again. "Tonight's the anniversary of when I was assaulted. If this is the man who attacked me and has targeted me again because I was the one that got away, what better night than tonight."

TJ kept quiet. Her logic made sense, but he questioned whether a killer would actually be stupid enough to hike to the top of a waterfall in the middle of a snowstorm.

The roads weren't bad yet and the heat from the previous days kept the flakes from sticking. Thank goodness for small blessings.

They pulled up to the Blue Ridge Parkway gate. A white truck with green lettering was parked to the side. His friend stepped out and approached his vehicle. "I don't like this one bit, TJ."

"Neither do I but we are chasing down a murderer who we believe has a victim with him. I wouldn't even ask if it wasn't a life-or-death situation."

"The life-or-death situation may be you. Temperatures are dropping and the forecast is calling for three feet now in the higher elevations. In case you didn't know, that's us."

"We don't expect this to be easy, but like I said we have to find this guy."

The man hesitated, then moved to the gate and unlocked it, letting TJ through. He returned to his window. "Be careful. This blizzard is moving in fast and I don't want to find two frozen corpses in the morning."

TJ nodded and entered, hoping that his friend's words didn't come true.

Leila's watch flashed a little past three in the afternoon although with the thick trees and gray clouds hanging low, daylight seemed more like dusk.

Snow swirled across her flashlight beam as she hiked on what used to be a paved path. Now covered with several inches of snow, she forged ahead taking in the quiet. No cars, or road noise, even the animals had hunkered down for the storm.

If only she could stop and enjoy the winter wonderland unfolding around her, but instead a mixture of dread and desperation permeated her mind. What if she'd gotten the pattern all wrong and Dani wasn't anywhere near here. She'd put her and TJ's life at risk hiking during a massive snowstorm. There were so many more elements they were facing other than a crazed killer, like hypothermia, but right now all her snow gear and layered clothing kept her warm.

"Hold up," TJ said. "I forgot my radio and since we don't have cell service here, I need to go back and get it."

"I'll wait here for you."

"I think it would be safer for you to go back with me," he insisted. "I don't want to leave you alone."

Leila looked at the top of the steps they'd just descended from the parking area. "The car's right there. No one's going to bother me while you are only a few feet away."

"Fine. But don't go wandering off on your own. We don't know where Pete is or even if he is here. However, if he knows you're coming for Dani then he'll be close."

TJ paced away from her and Leila looked up at the trees as the snow fell on her face. All her surroundings were cloaked in white as if God wanted to wash away the dirt of the world the same way He'd given her a fresh start. She needed His guidance more than ever right now.

A car door slammed above her. TJ stood at the top of the staircase, radio in hand. Then a small, muffled noise sounded behind her. She pivoted and stepped forward. "Dani?"

She inched forward around the bend, searching the thick forest for any sign of her sister. Maybe she had escaped and needed help.

"Dani?" she said again, a little louder.

"Leila, wait." TJ's voice reached her ears but she ignored his distant warning and rushed ahead faster, breaking into a jog.

If her sister was up there, she couldn't wait. The path narrowed and a thick canopy of trees hung over her draped in winter, creating a white tunnel. She continued forward alone, then stopped to listen. Something rustled behind her, off the trail. She turned but a powerful arm lashed out, clamping over her mouth and pulling her backward into the tree line. She thrashed, but her assailant was too strong.

He extracted her weapon from her hand, slammed her back against a tree trunk and pressed the gun's cold metal into her temple. He leaned the bulk of his muscular body against hers, pinning her into place. "Make a sound and you and your sister are dead."

Leila froze, staring into his cold, dark eyes. She knew him. He wasn't the man who'd tried to shove her into the van or attacked Holly in her house. But he'd injected himself into her life on a regular basis and she never even realized he was evil. How could she be so oblivious? A snow camouflaged hoodie covered his buzz cut and a mask hid his face. She closed her eyes and leaned her head against the tree. She should've never left TJ. What good would she be to Dani if he killed her here?

Leila's heart dropped as TJ's voice called out to her and faded as he moved forward on the marked path. He had passed right by them, oblivious to her location.

Her attacker stood a bit straighter, still keeping his hand over her mouth. "Like I said. Scream and you and your sister die."

He'd kill them anyway, but she wanted to see Dani. Maybe if they were together, they could take him since both were trained to bring down men twice their size.

He shoved her forward deeper into the trees, the weapon pressed into her back. She had to think, use her training. She was his hostage and she had to try to connect with him, buy her and Dani some time until TJ found them.

"You don't have to use the gun, Pete. Obviously, I'll go wherever you are holding my sister. I want to know that Dani's okay."

"Forgive me if I don't trust you."

"On the contrary, I talked to you every day. You even helped me when I ended up at the bottom of the ravine." She hesitated a moment. "Or were you the one that put me there? Someone must've seen you and that's why you loaded me onto your golf cart. If anything, you've broken my trust."

"Difference is, I don't care." He grabbed her arm, secured a piece of duct tape over her mouth and restrained her hands behind her back. "Pull any stunts and I'll kill your sister first while you watch."

She lifted her chin and didn't break his cold stare. He motioned toward the upper falls trail and she walked in that direction. At least TJ knew where Pete would be taking her. Hopefully, he'd continue in that direction and she'd find Dani before they reached the top.

"Keep moving," he said. "Time to join your sister."

Leila's bound hands were numb due to the tape being wrapped tight around her wrists. At least she was wearing gloves to help with the cold. Snow fell heavier and made the trail difficult to follow. Wind whipped around them and stung her face. The man had to be cold. He had on a toboggan under his hoodie and a thin coat over that.

He stopped and leaned against a tree, then reached up and ripped off the tape from her mouth. Her skin burned from the sudden detachment but she wasn't about to let him know he caused her any more pain.

"We're close to the river now. No one can here you scream over the rapids." He wadded the piece of tape into a ball and shoved it into his pocket, then handed her a phone. "What's Holly's number?"

Leila glanced at the phone, then back to him. "You kidnapped me so you could get my sister's number? Not really the way you want to win a woman's heart."

"I'm not going to talk to her. You're going to text her. And you're going to tell her to meet you and Dani at the farm."

His instructions alarmed her. The last thing she wanted to do was have all her sisters head to her mother's house. "I'm not going to do that."

Again with the gun. "Yes, you are."

"Why not let Dani go? You have me. I'm the one you've wanted all along, right? If this is about what happened that night at the bar, then let's figure this out. She's not a part of this."

"Give me Holly's number or Dani dies."

He turned his screen for her to view a live feed of Dani tied up. "There's a guard with her. If you don't do as I say, I'll give him permission to put a bullet through her skull."

Leila obliged, not sure what he had planned for the three sisters. After he hit Send, he said, "I don't know anything about a night at a bar." He shoved her forward. "Keep moving."

Leila headed back up the trail with Pete behind her. She tried to make sense of his words and the reason he wanted her family at the farm.

She scanned the woods for any sign of TJ. He had to be going in the same direction unless he'd gone back to look for her. If that were the case, then she and Dani would be on their own with a madman.

TJ searched the snow for any of Leila's tracks but they'd disappeared with the blizzard-like conditions. Surely there was something to indicate which way she'd gone.

He rushed back around the bend and surveyed the area for any evidence of her location. How did this guy abduct women so quickly even when others were around? TJ was right behind her and now she was nowhere in sight. The snow fell so hard and fast that in a matter of seconds, there would be nothing to show where Leila had been taken.

He didn't have much time but there was one barely visible indention in the snow that led off the path and into the woods. TJ stood at the edge, staring, listening, but only the nearby roar of the river met his ears.

If Leila was correct, then Pete would take them to the upper falls, and TJ didn't plan to let her join the multitude of photos the news stations played at eleven o'clock.

He inhaled and concentrated through the haze of exhaustion cloaking his mind. He had to stay focused, stay sharp. With a quick turn he was able to make out the trail again, but the terrain was much steeper and full of rocks. Even on a good day this part of the path was a challenge but with darkness all around him and snow at least six inches deep now, the climb was even more treacherous.

TJ slipped. He stumbled down a steep embankment but stopped the forward momentum with his strong grip of a tree trunk. He held there until he got his feet turned back around and managed to return to the path without injury. He hoped Leila was doing her best to give him time to catch up, but if she knew Dani was at the other end, she'd rush to be by her sister's side. He didn't blame her. If he'd been there when his father faced his murderer, nothing would've stopped TJ from doing the same.

He continued forward. The roar of the water

grew louder as if spurring him to the top. He quickened his pace and ignored the burn in his legs.

The tall evergreen trees cleared and his feet stepped onto solid rock. The river ran to the right of him and disappeared over a fifty-foot drop straight down. The problem was, neither Leila or Dani were there.

TEN

The frigid air bit through Leila's layered snow clothing, doing little to shield her from the bone-chilling cold. Evergreen trees loomed on all sides, their branches heavy with snow. Up ahead, the path split. The left fork led toward open fields that once held hundreds of tree trunks, giving Graveyard Fields its name. To reach the upper falls, Leila guessed they'd continue straight. Perhaps TJ waited for them there, ready to intercept.

Pete yanked Leila to the left, the gun pressing into her back. "This way."

"But the upper falls are straight ahead."

"If we were headed to the upper falls, we'd go that way. We're not."

Leila's stomach dropped. She'd told TJ the killer would have Dani at the upper falls. She'd been wrong. He was changing his pattern, making their survival even more uncertain.

Leila stumbled along the trail, her hands bound tight behind her. She risked a glance over her shoulder but saw no sign of TJ. Fear pounded in her chest at the thought of being taken further from any chance of rescue. TJ wasn't as familiar with these trails—they hadn't done much hiking together when they dated. Once she started at the precinct, her career had consumed most of her time.

The path grew treacherous—rocky, uneven and slick with fresh snow. Leila's foot caught on something hidden beneath the white blanket. She pitched forward, unable to catch herself, her cheek striking a jagged stone. Warm blood trickled down her ice-cold skin and left a red stain.

Pete unleashed a string of curses, hauling her up with a rough grip and setting her back on her feet. "Watch it, honey. I'd hate for you to crack your skull and miss out on the main event."

He shoved her onward, further up the trail. Despite the quiet of the snow-muffled forest, the roar of rushing water diminished as they walked further from the falls. No way TJ would find her in time.

"Why are you doing this, Pete?" Leila asked. "What have I or my sister ever done to you?"

"Nothing. You and your sister hardly speak to me. I don't owe you anything, but I've got a bookie I need to pay by tomorrow. This side job is the only thing keeping me alive."

Leila's steps faltered. "You mean you're not the serial killer?"

"Afraid not. But don't worry, you'll meet him soon enough."

"Have you met him?"

"Not exactly, but I've figured out his identity. Years of working in security helps, I suppose. I'm no idiot."

"Aren't all puppets idiots?" Leila poked at him, hoping to provoke him into revealing more information.

Pete jabbed the gun harder into her back. "Don't make me kill you before he's ready. I'm no puppet."

"You're doing his bidding for money. Sounds like a puppet to me."

With each barbed remark, Leila tried to get a rise out of him, desperate to uncover the true identity of the serial killer. He hired desperate men to be the face of his operation, abducting women as his victims while he remained in the shadows. He was a coward, and Leila planned to tell him so when she stood in front of him. "You know he plans to kill us all, right?"

"Better you than me."

Leila's mind raced. "Did he give you a reason for all the murders he's committed?"

"Only one, which you'll find out soon enough."

"What about a hint? I'm going to die anyway, so it's not like it matters if you tell me earlier than planned. Come on, Pete. Shouldn't you grant a dying girl her last request?"

They walked on in silence for several minutes. Pete seemed to be weighing his options. "I never knew my biological father," he finally said. "Had a stepdad who was...less than kind, to put it mildly. I've been married and divorced three times. My kid won't talk to me. And the man who's paying me? His story is even worse."

Leila seized on the opening, hoping to keep him talking. "How so?"

"Not my story to tell." Pete shoved her from the woods and into a clearing. Sprigs of grass poked through the snow-covered field. Wind whipped around them, stronger than the storm alone could account for.

The rhythmic thump of helicopter blades cut through the air. "This is the end of the line for me," Pete said. "Time for you to hop in the chopper."

"We can't leave in this weather."

"Shouldn't be a problem. The winds have died down, and he's a military pilot who can fly in all kinds of conditions. Now, move."

"Hence the blood wings," Leila said.

"Apparently, he followed in his father's footsteps."

Leila caught the emphasis. "Who's his father?"

A slow grin spread across Pete's face. "Enough with the questions. Get in, or I'll shoot you right here."

He shoved her again, and she stumbled but remained upright, moving toward the fuselage. As she drew closer, she could make out more details. In the back seat, a blonde woman peered out the window, her blue eyes a mirror of Leila's own.

Dani.

Leila's pace quickened. Amid all the chaos and fear, relief flooded her at the sight of her very much alive twin sister. She'd never been more thankful to see her sibling's face. A new resolve rose within her. The killer had finally made his crucial mistake. He had underestimated the lethality of the Kane sisters when united. The fight he had coming would bring either justice or death. His choice.

* * *

An hour later, TJ made it back to his truck, frustrated with himself. He'd watched the helicopter fly over as he stood at the edge of the upper falls. Leila had to be inside, and the killer had outsmarted them both. But TJ wasn't one to give up, not when it involved the only woman he'd ever truly loved.

He slid into the driver's seat, cranked up the heater and called Sergeant Quinn. His earlier attempts to radio had failed to connect.

"He's got Leila," TJ said, shifting into Reverse and executing a half doughnut in the empty parking lot. He grabbed the shifter and engaged four-wheel drive.

"What? How?" His superior's voice filtered through the vehicle's speakers.

TJ couldn't hold back, not with Leila's life in the balance. "She was convinced he took Dani to the upper falls at Graveyard Fields. Your team was too far out. We hiked into the area, got separated, and Pete grabbed her. Or at least I think it's him. Next thing I know, she's in a helicopter."

"Pete? The neighborhood security guard?"

"Yeah. Makes sense, really. He'd know each woman's jogging schedule, and he has easy access and an alibi if anyone ever came across him in a compromising position. He even acted like he was helping Leila the day she was attacked, when it was him all along, which threw us off his trail."

"He's our killer?"

"Looks that way. Though I didn't get a visual ID on him at the falls."

Silence punctuated the call. "So you didn't see him? Not once?"

"No, but we have photos of him with Dani and Leila on hiking trips, as well as with Kitty St. Claire. I'm sure he's the one behind the abductions."

"That tracks. He had access to the entire neighborhood and alibis through his job that could cover him."

"And his mom lives in the wealthy area. He was with Leila when the assailant first tried to grab her. I thought he helped her escape, but if he's the killer, he could've been the one who attacked her to begin with, then made it look like he was helping when I drove up."

TJ navigated down the mountain, his truck fishtailing as he took the curves too fast. He downshifted to slow his momentum. The last thing he needed was to end up at the bottom of a mountainous ravine.

"Can you get a helicopter in the sky?" TJ asked. "It's the only way I know to track her."

"As soon as the weather breaks, I can."

"This will all be over by the time the weather breaks. If you want Dani and Leila to have a chance, we need someone willing to fly in these conditions."

"That goes against policy, but I'll see what I can do. Got a friend who used to be a military pilot. He owes me a favor."

TJ ended the call and continued down the winding Blue Ridge Parkway. He had no idea where Pete might be taking Leila, but if he didn't find out soon, she was as good as dead.

As he drove, TJ's mind raced through possible locations. The killer had a pattern, a method to his madness. He'd taken the women to remote areas, places with significance. What did he know about Graveyard Fields? It had gotten its name from the stumps and logs left after a massive logging operation, their appearance reminiscent of gravestones in a field.

TJ pulled over, grabbed his phone and began searching for information on the area's geography and history. He scrolled through pages of information, looking for anything that might connect to the killer's pattern. Why would he need a helicopter, though, if he took them somewhere else off the Blue Ridge Parkway? Maybe dumping the other bodies here was a way to keep them focused on the wrong location.

TJ put the truck into gear and called Sergeant Quinn back. "He's not on the parkway."

"But he's dumped every victim's body there in the past couple of months. Why would he change now?"

"To throw us off track. I need to know where that helicopter landed. Can you get me any information on that?"

"Let me make a few calls."

"Great. Let me know as soon as you find out anything. Until I hear different, I'm headed toward the Kane family farm. Maybe Leila's sisters can help me locate them."

TJ ended the call and pressed down on the accelerator. The SUV's engine roared as it descended the winding mountain road. Snow was falling harder now, reducing visibility. TJ leaned forward, straining to see through the windshield.

As he rounded a sharp curve, his headlights illuminated a figure standing in the middle of the road. TJ slammed on the brakes, the truck sliding on the slick surface. He cranked the wheel, trying to avoid a collision.

The SUV fishtailed, then began to spin. TJ fought for control. He was able to get the vehicle stopped right at the edge and the figure didn't move. Just stood in the road staring at him. TJ stepped from his SUV, his weapon aimed. "Hands up where I can see them."

The man complied and walked forward, his footsteps crunching in the snow. He wore a snow camouflaged hoodie with a thin jacket. He pushed the hood back from his face when he got closer. *Pete.*

"Well, well," the man said. "Looks like the cavalry didn't make it in time."

"But I've got you. Hands on your head and turn around." TJ pulled his arms down one at a time and cuffed the man.

"Don't worry. You'll get to see your precious Leila one last time. The boss wants you there for the grand finale."

TJ pushed Pete into the back seat of his SUV and slammed the door closed. He had failed Leila. And now, they would both pay the price.

ELEVEN

Leila's heart pounded as she took her sister's bound hands in hers. One of the killer's henchmen cut the duct tape from Leila's wrists before buckling her in tight and restraining her once again. As Leila shifted in her seat, she felt something hard poking against her backside. A spark of hope ignited in her chest as she realized her key ring with the slim box cutter was still attached. If she and Dani could find a moment alone, they might have a chance to retrieve it and escape.

Leila leaned to the side and tried to get a good look at the pilot behind the tinted face mask of his helmet. He reminded her of the enemy pilots in popular military movies, but this was no film. The stakes were real, and the danger, palpable.

"My father was a paratrooper in the army," she said. "He rode in a lot of helicopters and jumped out of just as many."

The man remained silent, focused on steering with his cyclic control. Leila's gaze dropped to the man's chest, where a set of blood wings was pinned to his shirt. The sight sent a chill down her spine as she realized it was in the exact same location as all of his victims.

"I see you were a paratrooper too," Leila continued. "The pin you're wearing, my father had one just like it. Did you know him?"

The pilot dipped down over the mountaintops, following the river toward her family farm. After a moment of tense silence, he spoke. "I met him once. I wasn't impressed."

Dani leaned toward Leila, her voice barely above a whisper. "What are you doing? Are you trying to provoke him?"

"Trying to get information to help when we land."

"Quiet." The command came loud and firm from the pilot. He dropped the helicopter lower, flying into an industrial building several miles from the family home. As they touched down, the pilot unbuckled and removed his helmet, revealing his identity.

"Mackey?" Leila and Dani exclaimed in unison, shock evident in their voices.

He stepped from the helicopter and pulled

open the back door. "Get out," he said, his tone not tolerating an argument.

As they complied, Leila took in Mackey's imposing figure. He was bigger than she remembered, or perhaps seeing him in a small coffee truck each day had skewed her perception. Standing over six feet tall with two hundred pounds of toned muscle, he cut an intimidating figure. His dark hair was pulled back into a man bun, and the scent of coffee beans wafted past her.

Inside the hangar, a fifth-wheel camper sat in the corner, hooked up to water and sewer lines. Several vehicles were parked inside—a couple of coffee trucks, a large jacked-up truck with mud tires, a second burgundy van that hadn't been wrecked and a sleek, black sedan with tinted windows. Keeping his weapon trained on them, Mackey marched them toward the car and popped the trunk.

"Get in. Back to back."

Leila exchanged a quick glance with Dani, who had a severe phobia of tight spaces.

"Can't we get in the back and lie down in the seat?" her sister asked.

He pressed a gun to her head. "I said get in."

Leila gave her sister a subtle nod to go first. Dani crawled onto the carpeted floor and curled onto her side, then Leila followed suit with her back to her sister. She scanned the area, searching for taillight slots and safety latch releases. She knew their chances of escape were slim if she couldn't free their hands.

Mackey's voice dripped with malice as he spoke. "I bet your daddy never meant for you two to end up like this." Before Leila could respond or ask what he meant, he slammed the lid down with a sickening latch.

Silence engulfed the cramped compartment for a few seconds before Dani broke it. "Lei, what did he mean by our dad?"

"I have no idea," Leila said, a knot forming in her stomach. "But I've got a bad feeling we're about to find out." She scooted back until her back pressed against her sister's. "Can you reach my back pocket?"

"I think so."

"I've got a key ring there with a flat box cutter on it. If you can get it out, I'll be able to cut our hands free. Then we can work on getting out of here."

Dani shifted, her fingers searching. After a moment, she spoke again. "I've got the blade pushed up. You want me to try and cut your restraints first?"

"Yeah. Try not to slice my wrist, okay?"

Leila felt Dani's fingers touch the tape, followed by the pressure of each slice. "If you can just get it perforated, I should be able to pull it—"

With a final tug, Leila's hands ripped free. She flipped herself over, bumping her head on the trunk lid a couple of times before managing to cut through her sister's restraints as well. "Help me search for a safety latch to open this lid."

Dani grabbed her hand, her grip tight. "Wait. Be quiet."

Footsteps thumped next to the car, then the driver's door opened, and the engine roared to life. Dani released her hand. "Wait until we get on the road. If we bail out while in the hangar, we won't be able to escape. But when he slows down on the road, we can jump out and run through the woods."

"Good idea. Scoot around this way, and you can check the left side while I check the right."

"I'd give anything for a light right now. It's pitch-black in here and really cramped."

"Keep taking slow deep breaths. We're gonna get out of here. We'll have to make do with feeling around with our hands." Leila's finger probed the carpeted interior.

The car accelerated, tossing Leila to the side

as Mackey rounded a curve. "He must be on the main road now," she said. "We don't have much time. If he's taking us to Mom's, we've got about three miles before he's there."

"You know if we bail, he'll still go to Mom's house and round up all our family." Her sister's voice was laced with worry. "He's not going to stop when he finds us missing."

"We won't get that opportunity unless we figure a way out." Leila's fingers wrapped around a plastic hook. "I think I found it."

"What about Mom and our sisters?"

"He's going to round them up either way, right? This way, we get them out while he's searching for us."

Dani squeezed her hand. "You sure this will work?"

"It has to. We don't have any other choice."

Her sister exhaled a deep breath. "Then pull the trigger."

Leila waited for the car to slow at the last stop sign before her mother's road, then jerked the handle with all her might. Their escape time was now or never.

The fluorescent lights buzzed over TJ's head as he sat across from Pete in the interrogation room. TJ fought the urge to reach across the table and strangle the man, but he knew the greater justice would be to put him behind bars for the rest of his life.

"Petey, Petey, Pete. I have to admit, you had me fooled."

Pete's face remained impassive. "Apparently not fooled enough, or I wouldn't be here."

TJ leaned forward, his eyes boring into Pete's. "We have records that indicate you were working on the east side of the subdivision when victim number one was abducted. We also have records that you were patrolling the area on the west side of the subdivision when Kitty St. Claire was also abducted. And of course, you and I both know you were there when Leila was taken."

"It's called working, Officer. Those were the areas I was stationed at on those days. The fact that the women went missing from those areas is merely a coincidence."

"Except for the fact that we've found your DNA on the clothing of all three women. And your manager said you're the one who makes up the schedule. A task you requested to do to help take the load off of her." He paused for a moment to let the man process the details. "So if you're the one who killed the women, now's the time to confess, or if you were merely passing them off to someone else and being the front man, then now is the time to give up the name of the man behind all this."

Pete's demeanor shifted, a flicker of uncertainty crossing his face. "I didn't kill them. Kieran Murphy grabbed the victims off the street and I helped secure the victims in the van until we made the drop. After you arrested Kieran, I stepped into his role."

TJ's eyes narrowed. "And you coordinated the abductions by letting Kieran know the best time." He placed a financial sheet in front of him. "We also have records showing the two ten-thousand-dollar deposits made to your account on the days the women were abducted. That's conspiracy to commit murder at the very least and when we uncover the text messages from your cell phone, I'll have enough to arrest you for murder one. However, if you tell me who's behind all this and where he took Leila and Dani, then maybe there is a plea deal in the mix for you."

The man's face paled when TJ confronted him with all the evidence needed to pin every murder on Pete. His future was going to be a ten-by-ten cell with bars. To give time for the facts to sink in, TJ paced to the two-way mirror and stared at his reflection. "Where's he taking her?" TJ asked, pivoting back toward the table.

Pete remained silent.

Heat rose in TJ's face as he struggled to maintain his composure. "Where did he take Leila and her sister Dani?"

Pete shrugged. "It's not like we were buddies and wasted time playing video games together. He didn't tell me his plans past the helicopter. He gave me a job. I did that job. And now I get paid."

TJ leaned forward, his fingertips pressing on the hard metal surface of the table. "We've frozen your accounts. The money you received from a serial murderer will be confiscated."

"Then why would you ever think I would tell you where he's headed?"

Realizing he was getting nowhere, TJ straightened, grabbed the folder and stepped from the room, slamming the door behind him.

Sergeant Quinn met him in the hallway. "I'll send in Edwards, see if we can get more out of him."

"There's not enough time to get the information we need. We have to find Leila and her sister another way."

"Maybe her mother or other sisters have

heard something. If Leila was in danger, who would be the first person she'd reach out to?"

"Definitely one of them." They walked side by side into the bullpen. TJ threw his keys onto his desk and took a seat as they slid to the floor. Quinn picked them up and placed them back on the surface, his calm demeanor a stark contrast to TJ's agitation. "Her oldest sister, Holly. She'd be the first one Leila would call."

Quinn nodded. "Then reach out to her. See if she's heard anything. If she hasn't, contact the rest of her sisters. Go to the farm where her mother lives. Talk to her neighbors. Somebody else must know something. The sooner we find the connection, the sooner we find Leila and Dani."

After two hours of making phone calls, TJ was no closer to finding their location. None of her sisters were answering their phones, every attempt going straight to voice mail. Growing increasingly worried, TJ checked the cell tower records for all the sisters. To his surprise, each one had last pinged off a cell tower near the farm. A coincidence? Maybe they were all at their mother's, but it was the middle of the day, when most people would be at work instead of at their family home.

A sense of urgency gripped TJ as he grabbed his keys and coat and headed for the door. He passed Edwards in the hallway. "Did you get any more out of him?"

"Yeah. Our killer has a beef with Leila's late father. Some lingering resentment from their past."

TJ pivoted back toward the door, his mind racing with the implications of this new information. Edwards caught up to him. "What do you think you're doing?"

"Going to Leila's family farm."

Edwards handed off a couple of folders to another passing officer. "Not without me, you're not."

"I'm just going to talk to Lila Kane and a couple of Leila's sisters."

"And if this killer has a grudge, they will be his prime target. I'm coming with you."

TJ didn't argue further, knowing he could use all the help he could get.

"Message Sergeant Quinn," TJ said as they hurried toward the parking lot. "Tell him we need a SWAT team too. We can't take any chances with this guy."

The connection between Leila's father and their killer was the missing piece of the puzzle. If only he could figure out who had the connection. Then he'd be better prepared if Edwards was right and they were walking into a lion's den.

Rocky pavement cut into Leila's skin and burned her flesh with road rash. Her body rolled for several feet before soft grass spread out underneath her. She ached from the impact of her jump but didn't have time to linger. The lives of her sisters and mother depended on them. The sedan she jumped from stopped moving. Red taillights glowed and she waited for Mackey to back up or get out yelling but he remained in the car.

Dani, who'd jumped first, waved at her from the other side of the road, then clutched her other arm close to her torso. Pain filled her expression.

Leila shot across in the darkness to join her sister, praying Mackey didn't see her from fifty feet away. He was probably watching every move they made and trying to decide whether to shoot them on sight or continue with his plan.

"We have to move," Leila said.

"I'm not sure I can." Tears filled Dani's eyes as she sat on the ground. "My shoulder."

Leila crawled around to her sister's uninjured side and helped her scoot down the hill away from the road. A car door opened and footsteps clapped against the asphalt. Leila and Dani flattened their bodies into the tall grass of the bank hoping Mackey wouldn't come too close.

He stopped at the back of the car, slamming the trunk lid closed. "Don't think you're going to get away from me. I have your mother and sisters. If you're not at the house in ten minutes, then I'll strangle them one by one."

Leila had no other choice but to go to him or he'd kill them all if she and Dani didn't make it to the house in time. To be honest, she wasn't sure she could stop him, but she was going to try. At least this way, she could plan a counter attack.

Mackey walked back to the driver's door, slid into the car and spun off toward her mother's house.

"We have to hurry." Leila pulled off her outer shirt and fashioned a makeshift sling for her sister's arm. "I don't think your shoulder is broken. It's most likely dislocated."

She helped Dani get to her feet and they took the wooded trail that looped around the edge of the farm. As children, they'd used the shady path. Sometimes, they even pretended to be cops, searching for imaginary criminals. If only they'd known then what they knew now.

At the edge of the tree line, Leila held up her hand to halt any movement. She scanned the perimeter. "Looks like Mackey has three guards, two at the front and one at the back." She motioned toward the barn. "Mom still keeps Dad's rifles in the barn's gun safe. Let's go there first and see what we can find."

"Hopefully he left something small enough for me to handle with a dislocated shoulder."

"Can you do this? I know your shoulder must be painful. I can pop it back in for you if you want."

"I can make it to the barn, and then we can try."

"With the way you shoot, I doubt even a dislocated shoulder will throw off your aim but we'll find something. You're all we've got."

They stole across the backyard and around the side of the barn where they would not be seen. Leila opened the side door and quickly shut it back once they were both inside. The scent of fresh hay and fertilizer filled the open aisle. Her favorite horse stomped his hoof at her. Leila reached out her hand and caressed the white stripe down his nose. That was the only color on him other than cocoa brown.

"We may have to change your name, Espresso, after all this is over."

He stomped his foot again and she moved forward to the tack room where her father's gun safe was located. She used the only numbers that ever mattered to her father, his wedding anniversary date. When she was six, she'd asked him why he didn't use her birth date and the reason he told her rang even more pertinent now in this moment than ever before.

"I use that date to remind me how amazing your mother is. She forgave me and loved me when I made a huge mistake. I'll spend the rest of my life and every anniversary trying to make up for it."

But he wasn't here to make up for his mistake. Leila wasn't sure why, but she had a feeling they were fighting his battle. Despite his past catching up with them, somehow his words brought her comfort and spoke to the strength of their family's love.

Leila grabbed two shotguns and handed Dani the semiautomatic pistol with the full magazine already in place. Her sister's face was pale and she was clearly in pain.

"Want me to see if we can pop it back into place?" Leila asked. "I know a massage technique, a much gentler process than just jerking back into place. Won't even hurt. I promise."

Dani nodded.

"Here, take a seat." Leila rolled a leather stool in front of her sister. "Try to relax. It won't be easy but take some deep breaths."

She sat opposite Dani, on a stool as well. "Place your hand on my shoulder. I'm going to massage your muscles. Do your best to relax."

Leila applied steady downward pressure on her sister's arm and massaged the upper arm and shoulder muscles, rotating between them. The rounded part of Dani's humerus protruded forward.

"Does that hurt?" Leila asked.

"It's bearable."

After a few moments, the head of the humerus slid right back into place. A smile crossed Dani's face. "That's better. The pain's gone."

Leila retied the makeshift sling. "Good. But keep your arm in the sling. Once it dislocates, it can happen again until it heals properly."

"Then I guess I'll stick with the Glock," Dani said, holding out her good hand.

"I doubt Dad ever thought he'd be having to engage in a turf war on his farm. He's got more in the house, but until we get inside we won't have access to those."

"You know if we could make a diversion, then Holly, Sasha and Chelsea know exactly where the goods are located. We need to buy them time to get to them."

Leila strapped on a cross-body ammo pack and filled it with extra buckshot. "Don't worry. When I let loose the first round of bullets, I have a feeling that will buy them time."

"We need to get in there. Any ideas on how you want to do that?"

Leila grabbed the tranquilizer gun her father used when the bulls got loose. "I think we need to take the rear guard out quietly. How good is your aim with this?"

Dani smiled. "I think I can manage."

The sisters slipped back out the side barn door and stuck as close to the house as they could by rounding the edge of the tree line to the back patio. The rear guard was sitting in one of their chaise lounges, seemingly mesmerized by the fountains in their pool. Dani was the best shot of all of them. She practiced daily and had won multiple national shooting competitions. She moved into the bushes along the fence line, the dark foliage camouflaging her location.

Leila crept through the dense tree line surrounding her mother's house to get closer to the lattice ascending to the second floor. If she could make it there, the element of surprise would be an advantage in confronting Mackey. He would expect her to come through the main or back entrance but not from inside or down the staircase. Leila waited for Dani's signal.

The back door opened and Mackey stepped out onto the patio. Leila raised her shotgun. She needed to be closer or she ran the risk of not hitting him at all. She figured there would be a contingency plan if something happened to him. Another hired hit man to finish what he had started.

"Anything back here yet?" Mackey asked the guard, who now stood as if he were at attention.

"No, sir. All is quiet."

Mackey looked at his watch. "Their time is up."

Adrenaline pounded through every fiber of Leila's body. If they didn't hurry, one of her sisters was going to die.

TWELVE

Leila stood on the second-story roof of her childhood home, her heart pounding in her chest. Relief washed over her as Dani gave her the all-clear signal, confirming that the rear guard was unconscious. Even with a dislocated shoulder, her sister remained the reigning shooting champion of their family. Leila ensured Dani's path to the basement door was clear. Their plan was for Leila to descend from the second floor while Dani surprised them from the basement. They synchronized their watches, each having two minutes to get into position.

As Dani disappeared inside, Leila shimmied her old bedroom window open and climbed through. The familiar scent of her youth hit her like a wave. Still boasting purple lavender paint on the walls, obscured by magazine posters of boy bands, she inhaled the sweet perfume scent lingering in the carpet and draperies. Her lava lamp, also purple, remained on the dresser her dad had crafted when she was twelve. A pang of longing struck her heart—what she wouldn't give to have him here now.

Inching toward the hallway, Leila peeked through a crack in her bedroom door, scanning for any movement outside. Only the glow from a living room lamp illuminated the area beyond her room. She got into position and glanced at her watch—thirty more seconds. Her plan was to create a diversion, keeping Mackey and the guards busy while her sisters and mother escaped to the basement with Dani and out the side door.

With careful steps, Leila crept down the hall to the edge where the wall ended and the banister began. The scene below made her blood run cold. Mackey had each of her family members seated on the floor, their hands duct-taped behind their backs, legs straight out front. He stood near the curio cabinet where her father's flag and bullet pin were displayed.

"I hope you enjoyed all the pins I left in honor of your husband." Mackey's voice carried up to her, dripping with malice. He walked over to her mother, helped her to her feet and then pushed her down into a kitchen chair. All of her sisters could see her.

Lila Kane did not respond, her face a mask of stoic defiance.

"I see you're the quiet type," Mackey continued, his tone mocking. "Well, let me explain what your husband did to me. I am his son. His only son. But because of you, he rejected even knowing me."

Leila's stomach turned at the thought. This man was claiming to be a blood relative, fathered by her dear old dad, and now turned into a serial killer. The revelation shook her to her core, but she forced herself to focus on the task at hand.

"We didn't reject you." Her mother's voice was steady, despite the situation. "We tried to get rights, joint custody with your mother, but she refused. She gave your father an ultimatum. He had to leave me and the girls if he ever wanted to spend time with you. We had been married for fifteen years, and although we went through a rough patch where he strayed, we were able to forgive each other and work through our difficulties. I believe we can do that with you as well, Mackey. I'm sorry your mother didn't give you the opportunity to know your father."

"Lies. Nothing but lies," Mackey said. "My mother told me the real story. That my father wanted nothing to do with me. That he was ashamed of me."

Leila raised her shotgun as Mackey paced away from the group toward the front entrance. If he moved just a little to the left, she'd have the perfect shot, and this nightmare would be over. But instead, he pivoted on his heel and faced her mother again. "But since he's no longer with us, I guess we'll never know."

Leila lowered the shotgun, her gaze falling to her mother's shocked expression.

"He wasn't ashamed of you," her mother insisted. "He loved you."

Mackey stepped behind her mother's chair, his fingers wrapping around her slim neck. "But he loved you more and had a family with you. All these girls. I could've been a good son."

Leila's foot landed on a creaky floorboard as she stood on the top stair. Mackey's gaze snapped to her, an evil smile stretching across his face. "You decided to join us."

"Let her go, Mackey," Leila said, her voice steadier than she felt.

"If you shoot now, you might hit your mother, and I don't believe you're going to take that chance."

He was right. She couldn't risk it. Instead,

Leila shot a look to Holly, sitting closest to their mother, then aimed up at the large deer horn chandelier hanging from the vaulted ceiling in the living room. She fired her gun, and the massive light fixture came crashing down. Holly and Chelsea grabbed their mother and pulled her to safety.

Leila raced down the stairs, aiming at Mackey as he ran for the hallway. She hit his leg, and he fell, but managed to return fire. A searing pain erupted in her torso as one of his bullets found its mark. Leila grabbed her side and collapsed to the ground. Sasha was at her side in an instant, pressing on the wound.

"Get everyone to the mudroom," Leila said.

Dodging bullets, Dani appeared from the basement stairwell, providing cover fire so her sisters could reach safety. Sasha supported Leila, half dragging her across the living room floor.

"How bad is she?" Holly asked as soon as they were all inside. This room had been fortified as a safe haven when the house was built. Leila's body grew weaker with each passing moment. Her mother handed Sasha a hand towel. "Use this to help stop the bleeding."

As Sasha applied pressure to the wound, Lila punched a secret panel that opened to reveal a hidden arsenal. She distributed 9mm handguns to each of her daughters. "I know you have questions, but right now, we can't let your father down. He didn't teach you gun safety for nothing. The only way we're going to survive is to shoot our way out."

Leila could barely stand. The thought of holding a weapon and shooting seemed impossible. "Leave me and get out of here. I'll slow you down."

"Nonsense." Her mother's voice was firm as she took Leila's hand. "You're a Kane woman and God did not give you a weak spirit. He made you strong. Now you will get up, and we will get you out of this house. You hear me?"

Tears threatened to spill, and Leila nodded. She didn't want this to be the last time she ever saw her sisters or her mother. Her mother helped her to her feet. "Ignore the pain. Think second wind. Strong muscles. Now, let's go."

Sasha reached for the door and turned the knob. Then tried again with a stronger jerk. It would not open. "He's locked us inside."

Chelsea stepped over. "Let me try."

She gave the knob several tugs, but the door remained stubbornly shut. "Do you all smell smoke?"

Leila sank back to the floor and peered underneath. White smoke was seeping into the room. "He's going to burn the house down with us inside."

They were trapped, and time was running out. Leila knew she had to find her second wind, a way to get them all out safe and sound. She couldn't let this psychopath win.

"Stand back." Leila had the best angle on the door and she wasn't going out like this. Pushing past the pain, Leila rose to her knees and aimed her weapon at the door.

The room fell silent as everyone held their breath, waiting for Leila to take the shot. But before she could pull the trigger, a loud crash echoed from somewhere in the house.

"What was that?"

"I don't know." Her mother's voice was tense. "But we can't wait to find out. Leila, take the shot."

She steadied her aim and fought against the pain that threatened to overwhelm her. She took a deep breath, focused on the door handle and squeezed the trigger. The gunshot was deafening in the small space, and the door handle exploded in a shower of metal fragments.

Sasha pushed the door open. Smoke poured into the room as they stumbled out into the hallway. The heat was intense, and flames were already licking at the walls of the living room.

"Stay low," Sasha called out, helping exit the room.

They moved as quickly as they could through the smoke-filled house, the sound of crackling flames growing louder with each step. "We can't get out this way. The front entrance is engulfed in flames."

The roar of the fire grew louder with each passing second. Leila could feel her strength ebbing away, the pain in her side becoming almost unbearable. Her strength buckled, and she collapsed to the floor, her breath coming in ragged gasps.

Lila Kane knelt beside her daughter, her face etched with concern. "You have to get up."

"Let's go out through the basement." Leila pushed up from her knees and held on to Sasha's shoulders for support as they descended the stairs. The group moved together through the basement, navigating mounds of clutter that had accumulated over the years. Old furniture, boxes of forgotten memories and discarded toys created an obstacle course they had to overcome. The air grew thicker with smoke, making each breath a struggle.

Chelsea reached the outside door first, her

hand grasping the knob with desperate hope. She tugged once, twice, then a third time. Her face fell as realization dawned. "He's locked this one too."

The sisters exchanged glances, a silent understanding passing between them. Without a word, they raised their weapons, aiming at the lock. The sound of gunfire echoed through the basement as each sister unloaded their weapons, the muzzle flashes illuminating their determined faces in the dim light.

But as the last shell casing hit the floor, Leila's heart sank. The metal door stood unyielding, the lock intact despite their barrage. The bullets had left little more than dents and scratches on its surface. Once again, Leila had led her sisters into a death trap.

TJ's heart pounded as he raced around the curvy roads leading to Leila's family farm. The night was dark, but his mind was even darker with worry. Shots fired had been reported by neighbors, and there was no doubt in his mind that the killer they'd been hunting was behind the attack. As he rounded the last bend in the road before the main driveway, an orange glow highlighted the night sky. At first, he wasn't sure what to make of it, but as he got closer, the horrifying reality set in—the entire farmhouse was engulfed in flames.

Fire truck sirens sounded in the distance, a promise of help on the way. But TJ feared they might be too late. He flew into the driveway, slinging gravel as he braked to a stop. The heat from the inferno was intense, even from this distance. Without a second thought, he leaped from the car and ran toward the house. The back and front doors were impassable, walls of flame blocking any entry. There was only one other way in, and TJ knew he had to take it.

He sprinted toward the basement, his lungs already burning from the smoke that permeated the air. As he rushed down the bank, the roar of the flames grew louder, drowning out any other sound. Reaching the bottom door, he found it intact but hot to the touch. There were no windows, leaving him blind to what horrors might await inside.

"Leila, can you hear me?" he said, his voice hoarse from the smoke and fear. But the crackling inferno above swallowed his words, any potential response lost in the chaos.

Detective Edwards appeared beside him, carrying a door buster. With a nod of understanding between them, they swung the device and cracked open the basement door. A wall of black smoke billowed out, momentarily choking them both. TJ dropped low, pulling out his flashlight, and began to crawl across the floor. The beam of light cut through the darkness, revealing nothing but debris and smoke.

Then, barely audible over the roar of the fire, he heard a moan to his left. Hope surged through him as he turned in that direction.

"Leila, where are you?" he asked.

"Over here." Not Leila's voice, but familiar nonetheless.

As TJ inched closer, he saw Holly and Chelsea emerge from the smoke, carrying their mother between them. The woman was unconscious, her skin a sickly gray tone that worried him. Without hesitation he helped them outside, up the hill, and into one of the ambulances that had just arrived. The vehicle sped away within seconds, sirens blaring into the night.

Red lights flashed as two firefighters followed him back to the basement entrance. They were dressed in full protective gear.

His heart raced as they got closer. "There're three more inside," he said.

The two men entered the smoke-filled basement. Seconds ticked by like hours as TJ waited, every fiber of his being screaming for any sight of Leila. But he knew he had to let the professionals do their job. They weren't that far into the basement, but the fumes were so strong, so toxic. Most fire victims died of smoke inhalation before the flames ever reached them. He prayed that wasn't the case with any of the Kane sisters, especially Leila.

Sasha stumbled out of the basement, blood covering her hands. She stopped in front of TJ, her eyes wide with shock and fear.

"Where's Leila?" TJ asked, dreading the answer but needing to know.

Sasha's voice trembled. "They've got her, but TJ…she's in bad shape. Mackey shot her. You need to prepare yourself."

The words hit TJ with a force of despair he'd never experienced before. His whole body shook, knees threatening to give way beneath him.

A firefighter emerged from the basement, carrying Leila's limp form. Her sister Dani followed close behind, coughing and stumbling.

TJ's eyes locked onto Leila. Her skin was so pale, almost translucent in the flickering light of the fire. She was unresponsive, her lips a sickly hue that matched her pallor. Blood covered her clothes, a stark contrast to her ghostly skin. The firefighter gently placed her on a stretcher, and paramedics rushed her to the waiting ambulance that sped away into the night, carrying Leila—and TJ's heart—with it.

Unable to process the whirlwind of emotions, TJ stumbled to the edge of the tree line and dropped to his knees. "God, please don't take her from me now." He could barely get the words out. "Not when we were just starting to find each other again."

As he knelt there, battling waves of fear and despair, something rustled in the shadows behind him. Years of police training kicked in, and TJ pulled his weapon, rising to his feet in one fluid motion. Stepping gently through the underbrush, he followed a trail of red drops that led him straight back to a grouping of trees.

There, leaning against one of the trunks, sat Mackey—the man responsible for all this pain and suffering. He clutched his wounded leg, a makeshift tourniquet fashioned from a belt cinched tightly above the injury.

"Don't move," TJ commanded, taking another step forward, his gun trained on the killer.

Mackey looked up, a pained smirk on his face. "Where am I gonna go, Officer? She clearly hit my femoral artery. If I don't get to a hospital soon, I'll bleed out. This belt is the only thing keeping me alive right now."

TJ's finger tightened on the trigger. "I should leave you for the animals to eat."

"That wouldn't be very Christian of you, would it?" Mackey taunted, his voice weak but still dripping with malice.

"I don't know," TJ said, fighting a surge of hatred coursing through him. "God will sort out the sheep from the goats. Seems like a fitting end for you."

"Or you could do what your job requires and arrest me?"

TJ's mind raced. The thought of this monster potentially walking free due to some legal loophole or high-powered defense attorney made his blood boil. "So you can be set free and hurt more innocent people? I don't think so."

He dropped the aim of his weapon to just above the tourniquet and gripped it tighter. One shot. That was all it would take to end this nightmare once and for all.

"Officer Snowe." Sergeant Quinn's voice cut through the tension. "Cuff the man and read him his rights. We have a process, and you're not a killer."

TJ's hand trembled, caught between duty

and desire for vengeance. After what felt like an eternity, he lowered his weapon and holstered it. With mechanical movements, he handcuffed Mackey to a waiting stretcher. As the paramedics wheeled the killer away, TJ could only hope that true justice would be served and God would take his life, the same way Mackey had stolen so many others.

Fifteen minutes later, TJ arrived at the hospital, desperate to find Leila. He headed straight for the emergency room. The sight that greeted him nearly broke him—the four Kane sisters stood in the hallway, tears streaming down their faces. Several other officers gathered around spoke in hushed tones, their expressions grim.

A nurse passed by where he stood, and TJ reached out to stop her. "I'm here with the Kane family," he said. "A mother and daughter were brought in. Are both ladies on the same hall?"

The nurse's eyes softened with sympathy. "That's the daughter's room," she said, gesturing to a nearby door. "And I think the mother is down a few. Such a tragedy."

TJ's blood ran cold. "What do you mean, a tragedy?"

The nurse hesitated. "You'll have to speak

with the family, sir. I've already said more than I should."

As the nurse hurried away, TJ stood frozen in place. He knew, deep down, that the only tragedy in this case would be death. He stared at the group of sisters, not wanting to approach, not wanting to know the news. As long as he stood here, in this moment of uncertainty, Leila was still alive in his mind. He wasn't sure he could handle life without her.

Taking a deep breath, TJ steeled himself for whatever truth awaited him. With heavy steps, he approached the Kane sisters, each movement feeling like he was walking toward his own judgment. He prayed for the best but feared the worst.

THIRTEEN

Leila clung to TJ with every ounce of her strength, fingers twisted into the fabric of his shirt as if he might dissolve like a waking dream. Her body trembled against his chest from the grief of losing her mother and the trauma she'd endured.

"I'm so sorry." His deep voice rumbled against her ear as he held her close.

"I can't believe she's gone. She was fine, full of spunk and giving us orders, but the smoke was too much for her."

Her sisters had dimmed the lights to help with Leila's migraine and left the room when TJ arrived. He still smelled like smoke from the fire and a few bloodstains smeared his shirt. "Did you get injured too?"

He looked to where she pointed. "That's not mine. It's Mackey's."

Leila wiped her tears. "Did you find him?"

"I did."

"Is he dead? Please tell me he's dead."

He hesitated. "He's in surgery. You hit his main femoral vein and they took him straight to the operating room."

Leila tried to sit up but the pain in her abdomen was too much to bear. She rested back against TJ. "I want to talk to him."

"You need to rest. Just because the bullet grazed your side and there was no major damage, you still need to take it easy. Don't worry. There will be plenty of time to confront him."

"How…" Leila rasped out, her voice little more than a ragged whisper. "How did you find him?"

"You showed me the way," he said.

"How did I—"

"I was praying about you and there was a shuffle in the woods. I walked back and found him sitting underneath a tree with a belt fastened around his injured leg."

Leila leaned back into his arms. Every emotion swirled through her as she processed the fact that her mother's killer—and possibly her father's—was still alive right down the hallway. Adrenaline-fueled fire coursed through her at the thought of confronting him. She'd uncover every piece of evidence to make sure the man spent the rest of his life in prison. If not for her parents, then for the women who lost their lives to him.

"You found us at the farmhouse."

"I did."

"How did you know he took me and Dani there instead of the falls like all the others?"

"Detective Edwards figured out that he had a grudge against your father, so the only place that made sense to go was the farm."

His green eyes softened when she looked at him. "I'm so glad you found us, found me."

TJ's fingers brushed a strand of her blond hair from her face. "Kind of my job." He smiled and held her gaze. "I'm always here for you, Leila...no matter what."

Even after all this time after their separation, something inside her fractured at his gentle vow. She could deny the truth no longer. Tears burned afresh in Leila's eyes as she welcomed his lips on hers.

TJ pulled back. "You know, your mother told me that the secret to a lasting relationship was forgiveness. She mentioned that she and your father had gone through a rough patch but reconciled and forgave each other. I hope you can do the same with me and we can work things out for our future."

Leila leaned her head against his chest as they both sat on the ER stretcher together, her heart still broken over the loss of her mother. "I love you, TJ. Maybe I always will, but I need some time with everything that's happened." She fought back the emotions threatening to steal her voice. "My mom's gone. The farm is ruined and my sisters and I need time to figure out what we're going to do. Plus, I still have cases to investigate. This one alone is going to take most of my time."

"Oh. I see."

Pain flashed through his expression and anger filled her for the evil man who'd robbed her of so much. "I can't let Mackey get off on lack of evidence or a technicality. I have to make sure everything is done by the book so I can put him away for life."

TJ held up his hands. "I got it. Completely understand." He stood and moved toward the door then stopped. "You're going to be angry because it's part of the grieving process, but just don't let it take root in your heart. When you're ready, I'm here."

Leila stared at the wooden door to the private ER room as the barrier closed behind him. She'd done it again and pushed TJ away.

The next two weeks flew by in a blur. With her mother's funeral and the assessment of all the damage done to the house, she'd barely been able to think much less revisit the prosecutor's case against Mackey. They'd filed twenty-two felony counts against him including first-degree murder, arson and felony kidnapping, along with a slew of others. Leila consumed herself with work most days, but today the story Mackey had told her at the farmhouse kept nagging her.

She couldn't ask her mother what had happened. The evil man was her only source of any information but maybe she'd made a mistake coming to the jail for a visit. She fidgeted as she sat behind the glass panel that would separate her from the man who'd changed her life forever.

A loud buzzer triggered a metal door and Mackey shuffled through, dressed in a yellow jumpsuit and restrained with shackles on his wrists and ankles.

He took a seat across from her. "Took you long enough to visit your half brother."

"I'll need proof to believe that."

"Your mother should know all the details. Ask her."

Leila dropped her gaze to her hands, not wanting him to see the grief the mention of her mother triggered. "I want to hear your side."

"What's to hear? We share the same DNA but your father chose to raise you and neglect his only son."

"My father wouldn't do that—unless he didn't have a choice."

"I tracked him down two years ago but he wanted nothing to do with me. Even paid me to stay away so as to not upset your mother. How is she anyway?"

Leila wanted to wipe the smirk from his face. "I think you most likely know about my mother since you're the one who killed her."

He sat back in his seat feigning shock and placed a hand on his cheek. "Me? I don't know what you're talking about. I was with my girlfriend the entire weekend and she's willing to testify. You must be mistaken."

Heat flushed into Leila's cheeks. "Another one of your paid lackeys, I assume. You killed all those women and my mother. I'll make sure you pay."

"Horrible, isn't it?"

"What?"

"Not having a parent in your life. Now you know."

"Is that why you did it? To make me and my sisters suffer by taking the only parent we had left. That was your end game?"

"Not just your mother dear, but your father too. A shame how he died."

Leila sat up straighter, his words firing every nerve synapse. He wanted a reaction out of her and she obliged. "He died of natural causes— a stroke while he was in rehab."

"Is that what they told you? Don't you find it interesting that he was getting stronger and was almost ready to be released, but the night he died it was so sudden. Too bad you weren't with him like I was, when he took his last breath."

Leila slammed her palm on the counter in front of her. "You killed my father?"

"Let's just say if he didn't want to be my daddy, then he wasn't going to get to be yours either."

"And what about the other women? Why did you kill them?"

"Again, I don't know what you're talking about. I didn't know them."

Her phone vibrated. TJ had messaged her

wanting to know where she was. She jotted out a quick message telling him she'd call later.

The buzzer sounded again. Leila looked up to find Mackey's seat empty and the metal bar door closing. Their conversation was over but his words remained in her head locked in a prison of their own.

A gaping hole gnawed at her stomach and no amount of answers would ever fill the void of losing both her parents.

She stood, not sure what else to do or say, then walked back through security, gathered her things and exited through the lobby. The March sun was warm for the first time in weeks but Mackey's words still chilled her to the bone. Maybe he was lying and just trying to get into her head. If that were the case, then he'd done a good job.

"Leila."

She raised her gaze toward the male voice speaking her name. There, in the sunlight, TJ leaned against one of the brick walls flanking the entrance door of the prison. Peace washed through her at seeing his face. His presence gave her perspective. There was nothing she could do to change what Mackey had done, but her future stood right in front of her.

"How'd you know I was here?"

"I stopped by your house and your sisters told me. They were worried about you."

"And you?"

He shrugged. "I figured confronting the man who killed your mother and almost took your life was something you needed to do. You're strong and can handle yourself with him."

She dropped her gaze to the ground as Mackey's words rolled through her mind again, drowning out everything TJ said. Her father never deserved to die at the hands of a madman, especially one who claimed to be his son. She'd make sure to check with the district attorney and see if they could confirm her father's paternity. She had to know if Mackey was truly a blood relative, but somehow she knew he was.

TJ ducked his head to reconnect with her dropped gaze. "Are you okay? Did you talk to him?"

"He killed my father." Leila struggled to say the words, but TJ was the only one who could help her through the devastation of finding out the truth.

TJ strained to hear her and pressed up from the prison's outdoor brick wall, the rough texture scraping against his back as he straightened. "What did you say?"

Leila's demeanor sank with a mix of emotions—grief, anger and something else he couldn't quite place.

She inhaled, as if mustering up the courage to repeat the painful revelation. "Mackey went to my father's rehab hospital one night." Her voice trembled, but she pressed on. "My father didn't die of natural causes. The same man who took my mother's life in the fire killed my dad."

The weight of her words surged through him, igniting rage and sorrow for her and her family. Without hesitation, he wrapped his arms around her, pulling her close against his chest.

"I'm so sorry, Leila." His heart broke for the extra pain this man had caused. "How can I help?"

She shook her head against his chest, the scent of her lavender shampoo wafting upward while her fingers clutched the fabric of his shirt. "I wanted to break the partition and strangle him with my bare hands like he did all those other women." Her admission came out in a rush, raw and honest. "But then...then something happened."

Leila pulled back and met TJ's concerned gaze. "A peace came over me. Something steady and stable and inexplicable. I've never felt a calm like that before. It was like…"

"Like God was right there with you?"

"Yeah."

"I know how you feel. I had that same steady peace after my dad was killed. God was more physically real to me in that moment than any other time in my life."

She broke his embrace and took TJ's hand in hers, their fingers intertwining without thought. They walked toward the parking lot where her car was parked in the second row. The gravel crunched beneath their feet, a rhythmic soundtrack to the moment.

"How long did it last?"

"I still experience God's steady presence every day."

Silence filled the air between them as they walked. TJ let her process whatever emotions she was experiencing. News like she'd received today, even if the words came from a madman, were still life-altering. They stopped when they reached her SUV.

TJ motioned toward the prison. "I hope it's okay that I crashed your outing today."

"I'm glad you came." She let go of his hand

and ran her fingers through her hair. "My sisters didn't want me to come but this was something I had to do."

"I get that."

Leila glanced around the lot. "I don't see your car. How'd you get here?"

"Quinn dropped me off by the prison on his way to a police conference. He said you're in his thoughts and prayers."

Leila managed a small smile. "He's a good friend. We're blessed to work for him."

She fiddled with her key fob. "Do you think if Mackey had a better family, he would've turned out different? Made different choices?"

"You aren't blaming your father for Mackey's crimes, are you?"

"Of course not." Leila pressed the button on her key fob and opened her driver's-side door. "I just thought if he had someone who had loved him when he was younger or a family to take care of him like I have my sisters, would he have turned into a killer?"

"I don't think there's anything that will change a psychopath."

"Forgiveness can change people."

TJ's eyebrows shot up in surprise. "Letting him off the hook's a tall order."

She nodded, acknowledging the difficulty of

what she was proposing. "My parents taught us to forgive others no matter what. Doesn't mean I have to accept them or even speak to them ever again, but for my own heart, I have to extend the same mercy God has shown me." Her eyes searched his, seeking understanding. "It's not just about Mackey. I can't let this anger ruin the rest of my life."

TJ reached out, tucking a stray strand of hair behind her ear. "You're incredible, you know that? Your strength amazes me."

Leila tossed her bag onto the passenger seat. "I just don't know why he killed the other women. They weren't tied to my family in any way."

"Edwards texted me early this morning. That's why I came by your house." TJ took a deep breath, knowing the information wouldn't be easy to hear. "Your father had three good military friends who helped him cover up his affair. The three female victims were their daughters."

The color drained from Leila's face. "Those poor women. They probably had no idea."

TJ cupped her face in his hands. She was more beautiful today than ever, even with the sadness etched into her features. "I'm so sorry this has happened to you. I wish I could take all the pain away."

"Pain is a part of life, but God is bigger. I'll be okay. Just takes time." She offered him a small, brave smile. "And having you here...it helps more than you know."

Leila lowered herself into the driver's seat and started her car. The engine purred to life, a stark contrast to the heavy emotions swirling around them.

"I was hoping we could spend some more time together," TJ said, leaning against the car door. "You headed back to the farm?"

"Yeah. My sisters and I have to figure out what we're going to do about the farmhouse. We're meeting at Sasha's." She glanced up at him, a hint of her usual warmth returning to her eyes. "You're welcome to join."

"I was hoping you'd say that for two reasons—I need a ride home and I have something I want to show you."

He couldn't wait to show her the surprise he'd planned. Maybe that would put a smile back on her face.

"Oh? What kind of something?"

"You'll see when we get there."

"Really, TJ. You don't have to do anything—"

"You've been through so much in the last

few weeks and I just wanted to spend some time with you, outside of work."

"All right, Mr. Mysterious. Hop in and let's see what you've got planned."

The drive to the farm was filled with occasional comments about the scenery or memories of happier childhood times. As they pulled up to the farmhouse, the charred remains dampened their lively conversation. Leila slowed the vehicle and stared out the window for a moment, before continuing forward. "Where am I headed?"

"You need to go a little further unless you'd rather wait."

She faced him. "Of course not. I want to see the surprise."

"Then swap places with me so I can drive and you can close your eyes."

Leila raised an eyebrow but complied without any argument. He finished the drive, parked and grabbed what he needed from their barn, before taking her hand and leading her down the hill. The temperatures were perfect for what he had planned—sunny, but cold enough to keep the ice frozen. He planted her right in front of the pond. "Okay."

She opened her eyes. "Are you kidding? You

want to go ice-skating again? Don't you remember what happened last time we did this?"

"I think we need a do-over." TJ handed her some skates.

"A do-over?"

"Yeah. Something to relieve the heavy stuff for a little while."

Leila took the skates from his hands. "Where did you find these?"

"Your sisters got them from your house and stashed them in the barn for me. They think you need some fun too."

"You're unbelievable, you know that?"

TJ motioned to a bench, put on his skates and then stepped to the edge, holding out his hand. "Skate with me, Leila Kane."

She nodded and slipped her fingers into his as he tugged her forward through the crisp air. Their blades cut across the ice with a rhythmic slap. Leila spun around backward to face him, muscle memory kicking in despite the years since she'd last skated.

"You've been practicing," she said, a hint of her old playfulness returning.

"A little." But before the words floated into thin air, the tip of his blade caught in a divot and took both of them down, spinning across the ice.

Leila stretched out on her back and broke into a fit of giggles. Rays of sunlight streaked across her hair, making the strands look more golden than normal.

She flipped over, her face close to his. "You're right. I did need this. In fact, I need you."

He pushed to a sitting position, not waiting any longer. "I need you too." He closed the distance and pressed his lips against hers, tender and unhurried, savoring their moment of complete forgiveness. He let the past go with the physical promise of something new.

When they broke apart, a shout from the top of the hill startled them both.

"Finally." Dani's voice echoed around them.

Leila grinned and helped TJ to his feet, both of them a little unsteady on the ice. She looked up to see all of her sisters lined along the crest of the hill, their faces beaming with happiness.

"Did you invite them?" she asked, surprise and joy mingled in her tone.

"I did, but they were supposed to wait until I gave them the cue."

"What cue?"

TJ's heart pounded as his fingers wrapped around the small box still in his pocket. He knew what he wanted and the time had come to let Leila know too.

He dropped to one knee right there on the ice, pulled out a ring that sparkled in the sun.

"What are you—" Her hands covered her lips as she realized his plan.

"Leila Kane—" he held up the ring "—you're everything to me. My partner, my best friend… and the most beautiful gift God has given me." His voice cracked, fighting to hold back his emotions. "I don't ever want to be without you again. I love you. Will you marry me?"

Tears welled in Leila's eyes, happy tears this time, and she nodded. "Yes," she said, her voice barely above a whisper as she held out her hand. "Yes. I love you too. There's no other man I'd rather be with than you."

As TJ slipped the ring onto her finger, Leila's sisters launched into cheers and rushed onto the ice, slipping and sliding, as they came to smother the newly engaged couple in hugs and congratulations.

They had found a full life. This was love— patient, enduring and resilient. This moment, with Leila in his arms, surrounded by the warmth of family…this was everything.

* * * * *

Dear Reader,

Can you believe that *Mountain Murder Threat* is book number six with Love Inspired Suspense? These past years writing for you has been a dream come true. God has blessed the stories and I pray He has blessed your lives through them. Thank you for your support. I couldn't have done it without you!

Love in Jesus,
Shannon Redmon